THE
SASSAMON
CIRCLE

LOUIS GARAFALO

Outskirts Press, Inc.
Denver, Colorado

The Sassamon Circle
All Rights Reserved.
Copyright © 2008 Louis Garafalo
V3.0

Outskirts Press, Inc.
http://www.outskirtspress.com

ISBN: 978-1-4327-2066-7

Outskirts Press and the "OP" logo are trademarks belonging to Outskirts Press, Inc.

PRINTED IN THE UNITED STATES OF AMERICA

JOHN SASSAMON

1620 - 1675

THE FIRST VICTIM OF KING PHILIP'S WAR

PART ONE

JANUARY 29, 1675

LAKEVILLE, MASSACHUSETTS

CHAPTER 1

In January, in New England, the wind arrives icy and cold, traveling long distances from the Canadian north. It flies in high, clean and sharp, and paints the sky with deep black stretches interspersed with twinkling white lights. *"Nanummattin"* the Wompanoags call this wind and from its aerial view one could see the world below with a clear and unique perspective.

On this January night the wide expanse of Lake Assawompsett looked starkly white. It had been dusted by a recent snow that was molded into place by low temperatures. The lake had been frozen since late December. On this night, the moon spun off its soft, wide light and the stars and the lake surface dutifully reflected it back creating a special, crystal serenity.

But if one could have ridden the wind down and closer to the surface, one would have seen bits of activity. Tracks from the shoreline leading out perhaps a hundred yards to a tiny, dark interruption in the snow, the remains of a small fire. Around this spot were four figures, one of which appeared to be holding the arms of a second man. Another of the men stood off to the side of the circular patch and was scanning back toward the shoreline. The fourth man was

1

frantically smashing something - a log, a rock? – down against the black spot. At last he rose and said something to the man off to his side. For seconds there was no further movement. Then, the man whose arms were being held ripped free from the grasp and bolted towards the shoreline. He ran awkwardly and it was clear that his hands had been tied behind his back. The three men sprinted in pursuit. One of the chasers closed on the running man and threw a piece of wood at his feet. The wood caught the running man at his ankles, tripping him off his feet and knocking him face first onto his chest. The three men now surrounded their prey who remained in the same position on the ice, lifting his head slightly but not looking up. Seconds passed, inaudible words were exchanged. Then one of the three men took a small log, raised it high above his shoulders and brought it down with full force against the man's head. The men stared in silence, looked at each other, then each grabbed an arm and a leg. They carried the man back to the dark patch, a hole in the ice that they had made. They tipped the body upright then jammed it head first into the black water, finally pushing it by the feet and shoving the last of it under the surface. One of the men laid a blanket across the opening and all three of the men began kicking snow to cover it up.

CHAPTER 2

The day broke as October days do in New England, the night's coolness replaced by a sparkling morning warmth, dry, clean and brightly sunny. Arby found himself sweating as he made his way along the well-worn path, the weight of his unique load causing him more than a normal exertion. This was a special cargo, a gift he was told, for someone very important. He was instructed that the contents must stay a secret and that he was to tell no one of their delivery. He speculated, perhaps something for Tuspaquin, maybe even Philip. Maybe the governor himself?

Arby squinted deeply as he looked into the yellow-green brightness that was filtering through the woods, head high, directly into his eyes. He had made this journey many times, it being his regular task to roll his wagon towards Plymouth and meet his usual contact. Normally his cargo was lobster and many in Middleborough referred to him as "The Lobster Man". The Nemaskets, one of the many Wompanoag tribes, thought Arby to be special and called him by another name, "*Massa-ashaunt*" meaning "Great Lobster". In fact, Arby was special because, until the arrival of the English, the natives had never seen anyone quite like Arby. His eyes were small and were strangely focused,

3

his head oddly shaped and compressed downward into a wide, fat neck. He had the face of a child even though he was almost thirty years of age. His words were contorted, thick and difficult to understand, often monosyllables. Arby was prone to making rhythmic, guttural sounds and had a habit of lurching his neck forward, a snapping movement, like a bird pecking at an unseen bush, responding to some unknown stimulus.

The Nemaskets thought that Arby possessed some unspoken power that afforded him a unique rapport with the birds, the trees, the woods. As such, Arby had been allowed access to this unknown path, a path that went directly through their sacred burial ground, a place no Englishman knew about let alone ventured through. The Nemaskets thought that perhaps Arby spoke a language of the spirits, that he had found the path because he had somehow been chosen to find the path, that he might be in communication with their dead through his strange chanting and mannerisms.

Arby knew none of this. He had a childlike joy of being in these woods and he had come to realize that his regular trips along this path were of importance to certain people. Lobsters were plentiful in nearby Plymouth, could be plucked easily right off the beach and were thus a convenient source of food. But transporting them inland was problematic as they had to be kept alive in sea water. Arby's father was able to make him a special cart, an oversized wheelbarrow really, with big wheels front and back. More importantly, the container portion of the cart had been sealed with resin and pitch to make it waterproof. Finally, his father had equipped it with a hinged wooden cover that latched. It made for a heavy and cumbersome mode of

4

transportation but Arby was powerfully built, strong in the shoulders and legs, and he handled the load proficiently.

The most direct path to and from Plymouth went through the burial grounds. While his primary cargo was lobsters, Arby was often asked to carry packets and letters for delivery to his contacts. Many of these requests came from his friend, John Sassamon.

Today, Arby had received his normal load of lobsters and was then asked to carry something else, a wooden box perhaps five feet long and a foot wide. He did not recognize the men who asked him to carry the box but they told him that it was very important that John Sassamon receive it. The box was tied tightly with rope at both ends and in the middle. The men laid the box on top of the wooden cover and tied it securely to the wheelbarrow. After Arby tested the load for weight and balance he signaled okay. The men smiled widely at Arby, handed him a sweet cake for his trip, assured him of their appreciation, and sent him along his way back towards Middleborough.

The path narrowed now as it ran past a small brook, elevated on an embankment perhaps four or five feet above the streaming water. Arby moved easily along the path towards the brightness coming through the woods. Reflexively, he began his guttural chant, his head bobbing, moving to some internal rhythm. From the grayish green peripheral light Arby could now see a shadowy image emerging from the woods. Someone else was along the path, someone quite unexpected, someone Arby could not quite identify. Surprisingly, even on this radiant morning, the figure was covered by a large, oversized coat, full hat, and scarf around his face. Instinctively, Arby's chants grew louder, a combination of greeting and concern. The figure did not speak but took a step directly into the middle of the path. Arby's moans intensified and he was able to scream a command, "Out!" But the figure did not move. Five feet away now and Arby gave a strong push to his wagon, his head down from exertion, his means of protesting this intrusion.

The figure made a quick side step to the edge of the path as Arby trudged by him. Then, without warning, the figure hurled himself against Arby, knocking Arby and his cart down the embankment and onto the rocky stream bed. The ropes holding the box to the cover of the wagon broke free during the spill sending the box darting off to the left. The hinges of the hooded cover were also jarred loose causing the cover to unlatch and fly open, releasing a burst of briny water and screaming black lobsters.

Arby had fallen hard, face first down the embankment and onto the rocks that lined the creek. He was dazed, moaning from multiple pains, his face cut badly in two places, blood streaming onto his hands as he tried to raise himself up to his knees. All his efforts stopped as he took a thwack of a blow to the back of his head. The figure from the path raised his club again, contemplating another swing, then realized that his work was done. He paused a moment to be sure then moved to his left and picked up the box.

A single lobster climbed over Arby's hands in frantic search and, looking into the glazed, dying eyes, saw the final image of itself.

CHAPTER 3

He had known immediately, known without seeing, knew just by the sound. As his party approached the swiftly moving Nemasket River that parted the Muttock area he knew that a large waterfall would soon come into view. He was not an educated man but he knew the value of a water force, knew what could be done when such power was harnessed. As they rounded the river's turn he saw it, just as he had imagined it seconds before, a beautiful tumbling of five feet or so, thrashing up a white airy spray and sending a torrent of water on its way downstream. He moved a few steps closer then stopped to stare. His five companions jolted him back from his reverie barking over the din that they needed to move on up the hill towards the center of Middleborough. He followed them but halfway up the hill he stopped and looked back. He knew.

His name was Leroy Lapham. That moment, that special moment, still so clear in his mind, had occurred some twelve years ago now. He and his five companions had come from Plymouth hearing that a settlement was taking place inland near an area that had many lakes. There would be opportunities for a man to make a stake. Even now he recalled the trip with a sense of bemusement. They went heavily armed ... to travel to a place that they might peace-fully settle their families. They were concerned about their safety among the Nemaskets ... yet used two of them as guides. As they made their way through the rolling green woods west of Plymouth they were met by indifference from the natives. Some curious stares, some glimpses of acknowledgment. But mostly indifference. It had always puzzled him. The purpose of their journey was to find land to settle, land that by English standards, was the domain of the Nemaskets. Yet the Nemaskets seemed to have no re-gard for the land, no sense of ownership and, apparently, no sense of loss. Leroy had always found it strange that the same natives that had such affinity for the land had felt so little need to claim it as their own, thought the land to be communal, like the air and the wind and the sun, almost in-tangible, to be shared without claim.

How it all had changed in twelve years.

He stood on the stone wall that he had built right next to the side of the falls. He could look left and feel the tumbling power, the watery spray, and the darting rush of water fly-ing downstream. He had narrowed the falling water, funnel-ing it forward, by erecting a large earthen wall perhaps ten feet across the river. Behind him stood the main work building, a large barn-like structure made of earth and stone and heavy wooden planks. The basic business of his opera-tion was a sawmill. Leroy had been able to harness the power of the surging water by directing it through a large waterwheel that was positioned right below his feet. Through a series of gears and pulley-like mechanisms he had been able to attach any number of large saw blades that could be comfortably operated by two men. With the force of the water powering these mechanisms, his men were able to direct the saws with great force into the trunks of trees and generate consistent, uniform pieces of lumber and poles. In the budding development of Middleborough there was a great demand for such products and Leroy had accumulated significant wealth.

He squinted through the morning haze, looking over the falls, the waterwheel, past the side pond that had formed, and scanned across the way, up the side of the hill that led beyond to Middleborough. He could see his own image looking back at him from that momentous day, so many years ago, frozen now in his mind.

He was a stern man but this particular memory always brought a tight smile to his face.

Leroy turned and entered into the large work area. A couple of his men were furiously cutting into a wide pine trunk with two others offering steadying support. His son Charles, his middle son, was at the far side of the building, sitting at a large desk, holding a paper and gesturing with some animation. Seated beside him were two customers. They appeared to be Nemaskets. One of them was holding a wooden bucket, spinning it slowly, all the while talking to his compatriot. Behind them stood a tall thin man who appeared to be talking to all three of them simultaneously. He was well known to Leroy, in fact, well known in the local area. His name was John Sassamon and he served as the primary translator in many dealings between the native population and the English.

Leroy watched as the two natives each picked up a wooden bucket. He saw Charles talking past the two men directing his conversation to Sassamon. Sassamon, in turn, nodded his head, passed something to Charles in exchange, and then signed the paper that Charles was holding. As the natives walked ahead out the building's far side opening, Sassamon had one final word for Charles, a quick repartee back and forth, and then both chuckled in laughter. Sassamon quick-stepped out the opening to catch his friends while Charles ambled over towards his father, a huge grin on his face.

"Bloody Irish!" he said softly, still smiling.

Leroy paused for a moment letting the comment sink in.

"Which one?"

Charles shook his head gently and turned back towards the desk, his ink quill still in his hand. Soon he was instructing two of the employees, one English and one native, about where to stash some of the pieces of lumber. Leroy watched his son's confident mannerisms, his definitive instructions, boisterous and animated as befit a man so physically big. By any standards, Charles was a large man, broad in the shoulder and back, built wide and thick, with great strength of thigh and torso. Such strength was Leroy's gift to his sons, Charles and Arby.

In his mid-twenties, Charles had the bearings of someone born of privilege, of ownership, and he willingly asserted such status. This rankled his father no end, the assumption of a status that was unearned. And yet Leroy had to acknowledge that Charles was now the driving force behind the family business, had seen the opportunities for various products and had seen just how useful someone like John Sassamon could be in their distribution. Charles was many things that Leroy was not – outgoing, gregarious, comfortable among those of status. And educated. Charles knew figures and calculations and could express himself in writing. He could talk to people of power and influence in their own terms, without trepidation. Charles had traveled to Boston, had seen Harvard College – Sassamon had taken him – and still talked occasionally of becoming a lawyer. Perhaps a judge.

Perhaps a governor.

For now, Charles was certainly a successful entrepreneur, had advanced the family business confidently and in many directions. All of the family had benefited - Leroy, Arby, Charles and Leroy's youngest son, Thomas. But it troubled Leroy to watch his son, conflicted him. He admired Charles' confident manner, a manner that could be outright pompous and arrogant at times. He admired his son's ability to feel such confidence as his natural right, to assert such importance, a Lapham staking out such a bold claim on his surroundings. Leroy had planted the seeds of the family success through vision, through determination, through persistence. It had brought Leroy all that he had hoped for – security and satisfaction in his work, recognition of his talent.

But Charles had taken his good fortune and brought it to a place that Leroy could not comprehend, a foreign place, a place for others.

Charles was a man of *influence*.

Lost in his thoughts in the middle of his shop floor, Leroy stared blankly at his son. Together, they had built a business around wood and wood products, lumber and fences and poles. Wooden buckets and wheelbarrows. Axe and shovel handles. Things that men needed to master their soil and contain their animals and corral the things that they owned. Useful things, manly things … controlling things. And yet, the gnawing feeling of dissatisfaction was undeniable, the need to prick at his son, to humble him, to remind him of things that were so ingrained in Leroy and so unrecognized by Charles. Charles had become the things that Leroy had dreamed of … but had never respected.

The musings ended as they always did. Leroy moved over to the main sawing area to assist two of his men with a fresh trunk of maple.

CHAPTER 4

He felt the need to slick his hair just one more time. One more time – for perfection's sake. From force of habit. For good luck. Hopefully she would be there. He searched for a container of water, obsessed now, finally finding a water bucket near the goat pen behind the side door to the tavern. Three fingers scooped down and through then up to his temple and through his thick brown hair. Feeling relieved he took one more second to straighten the collar of his woolen coat, exhaled deeply, then pulled open the heavy oaken door of the Tamarack pub.

He saw her immediately.

Sarah Horton was the daughter of John Horton, the owner of the Tamarack. The Tamarack stood just off of the main road that ran from Middleborough, along the side of Lake Assawompsett, all the way to the port of New Bedford. The Tamarack was many things – a way station, a livery, a rooming house, a pub. But it was more than that; it was a hub, a place of exchange – of goods, of services, of ale and lagers, of current events, of gossip, of influences and innuendos.

Thomas Lapham loved the Tamarack.

As he stepped inside, Sarah looked up from the table that she was setting, an instant of recognition, a slight smile and a shy look away. His chest buzzed and he quickly slicked back one more time. She looked up again, maintained eye contact this time, the smile widening, slightly crooked, crystal blue eyes and creamy white skin, walnut colored hair hanging long down her back and tied with a blue ribbon. She began walking toward him.

Thomas twitched under his coat, energy welling inside him searching for a release, his lips turning themselves upwards.

He found her devastating.

Only a few feet away now, his body rigid and his eyes locked on her, he heard her soft voice.

"Edward has been looking for you."

A quick last look then she turned and walked back to the kitchen hearth area. His eyes followed her across the room, tall and lithe, hair bobbing, subtle curves. His moment of reverie was broken by a hand placed firmly on his shoulder at the neck line.

"Ah, Mister Lapham!"

The voice was unmistakable, the dark baritone smoothness of John Sassamon. In his other hand he held a dull gray pewter mug the contents of which were swirling dangerously close to the top. It was apparently not his first ale of the day.

"I was at your establishment today, sorry to have missed you. Your brother Charles was so kind as to convince me of the errors of my way and happily instructed me that a higher price for our transaction was in order. Thankfully, we are both reasonable businessmen."

Sassamon jerked the mug up to his mouth, drank deeply, then abruptly yanked the mug back down, a slight froth remaining on his upper lip.

"Your father was as cheerful as ever."

Sassamon took another quick drink, looked furtively around the room, grabbed Thomas' arm and pulled him closer.

"Your brother thinks that there may soon be a business transaction that I might assist you with. You know I value my relationship with your family."

Thomas instinctively pulled away wondering just which business transaction Sassamon was talking about. Charles had always thought Sassamon to be an intriguing character, an interesting conversationalist, an astute observer and a social rogue. "Useful" Charles would say. Conversely, his father was suspicious of Sassamon, thought him shifty and self-important, two attributes that were the antithesis of a blunt, unpolished man like Leroy Lapham. Still, even Leroy Lapham had to admit that a man like Sassamon played an invaluable role in spanning the two separate cultures that were interwoven between the English and native peoples. And Sassamon had found a meaningful activity for Arby.

Sassamon was what was referred to as a "praying Indian" that is, a native who had learned English through the study of the Bible and whose charge it was to spread the Christian message. He had worked closely with a man named John Elliot and had contributed greatly to Elliot's mission of translating the Bible into the various native dialects of the tribes resident in southeastern Massachusetts. Sassamon's commitment to Christianity was subject to question but his latent intelligence, erudite manner, and love of the written word were not.

To say that John Sassamon was an interesting character was an understatement. He had been born in the Boston area in 1620, arriving in the same year as the English. As a teenager he had come under the influence of John Elliot and worked closely with him on his translation project. He had even attended Harvard College. John Sassamon had a certain sophisticated bearing and that separated him from all in the community, both native and English. In a time where most people were not educated and learning opportunities were limited, Sassamon was proficient in English as well as a number of regional native dialects. Accordingly, Sassamon's skills were in communication and commerce and he readily trafficked in both.

Sassamon's base of operations was the Tamarack where he maintained an upstairs room. Rumored to be the husband of a native woman nearby, no one had ever seen Sassamon with his wife and he rarely talked of family. A few people knew that he had a daughter and son-in-law living in the Lakes area. Clearly Sassamon enjoyed the buzz of activity that was a daily swirl at the Tamarack, the arrival of visitors and patrons bringing news and gossip … and opportunities. Nocturnal and gregarious, appreciative of ale and lager, Sassamon moved easily in this, his preferred environment.

But there was something amiss with John Sassamon, something troubling, something almost sad. As befit his unique skills and his personal outlook, John Sassamon lived in a lonely world inhabited by many but with connection to few. His place in either native or English society was becoming ill defined. While he moved fluidly between both societies, it was increasingly apparent that John Sassamon was not really accepted in either one. As with his friend Charles Lapham, John Sassamon saw himself as an entrepreneur and as a man of influence, a "new man", a man that could help shape the emerging society of mixed cultures that might evolve into its own unique hybrid society. Unfortunately, a man on such a cusp seemed destined to be viewed with suspicion, with apprehension, to endure a certain isolation and solitude.

Thomas was relieved of his discomfort with the arrival of his friend Edward Horton. Sassamon nodded to Edward, saying nothing, gave Thomas a knowing look, then moved off to the bar rail. Thomas and Edward both silently followed his walk.

"Did I interrupt a big deal?" inquired Edward with a hint of sarcasm.

"He said he wanted to talk to me about something that Charles told him today. I have no idea what."

Thomas caught Edward's face, a suspicious smile taking hold, registering his doubt.

"No, really! I'm never sure what he and Charles are dreaming up. I specifically told Charles not to talk to him about our venture but Charles gets easily swayed. Sassamon gets him talking and ..."

One of the staff brought over two beers and the men sat down at a small table. Like Thomas, Edward Horton was nineteen years old and, like Thomas, experienced both the freedom and the responsibility that came with being the son of a businessman. They had been the best of friends for as long as either could remember and shared a number of interests most noticeably a love for hunting bear. Both were expert marksman and both had an appreciation for the craftsmanship of firearms. Physically, they could not have been more different. Thomas was built like his mother, tall, almost six feet, reed thin, with long, stringy muscles, all sinew and angles, athletic and swift of foot. Edward, on the other hand, was short and compact with a large head, thick neck, large forearms. The joke was that both appeared to more properly belong to the other's family based upon their physical characteristics.

They sat for a moment, comfortable in each other's silence.

"When are we going out again?" Edward inquired.

Thomas did not acknowledge the question, drank deeply from his mug.

"I want to make one more change and then I think we are ready. Give me another day or two. What's today ... Monday? Come by Wednesday afternoon, we can get things ready and head out first thing Thursday morning."

The two drank in silence. From the corner, Thomas caught sight of Sarah putting mugs away in a cabinet, felt his chest lightening, his mouth opening slightly, his thoughts drifting.

CHAPTER 5

L eroy was irritated. He was not a public man, did not like attention, had little use for public pomp, and less use for those that dealt in such activities. But he was to be honored today with a ceremony in the center of Middleborough and they were running late. Leroy had no use for tardiness and no tolerance for those that caused it. He was ready, Arby was ready, their wagon was ready, even Thomas was present to attend. All were dressed in finery, Leroy with a new waistcoat and breeches and Arby looked sporting in a woolen jacket. Even Thomas had on a new deerskin coat. Yet his middle son was nowhere to be seen.

Finally, the wagon came into sight, the surrey that Charles had made for himself at the mill. Leroy had to admit that the carriage was impressive, drawn by two horses, with a high, elevated seat from which he could see Charles waving. Charles' wife Rachel and their four children were inside the carriage. Gaudy, Leroy thought, but undeniably an attention grabber.

As they made there way into town Leroy could not help but think back to the first time he had been to the town and his decision to settle near the waterfall. Middleborough had grown since that day twelve years ago and had been recognized as its own legal town entity a few years ago. As the town had become more populated, the nature of the settlements had changed. His initial journey to Middleborough had taken him through many areas of native population including some areas that would be considered densely populated. But even twelve years ago there were many instances of empty dwellings, situations in which it appeared that the natives had abandoned their village. Leroy was soon to learn the devastating truth – the villagers had been decimated by disease, generally small pox or some variation thereof, from which the natives had no natural immunity. The sources of the disease were unknown but diseases seemed to strike with terrifying regularity, coincident with the arrival of strangers.

White strangers.

Four years ago he had lost his own wife Iona. Everyone recalled the arrival of the hunting party that stayed in the area for a number of days. Two of them were Frenchmen who had traveled a long distance from Canada and down through Maine. They had come by the sawmill for tools and provisions and because the townsfolk had pointed it out as a source of pride and economic interest. That had been in October. Within months, as if carried by the Canadian wind, a plague of sorts had struck the area bringing with it a deadly version of illness. Iona had succumbed as had three of his native employees. Inexplicably, he and his three sons had been spared. For almost a year he could not get another of the Nemaskets to work at the mill. For almost a year he blamed himself for exposing his wife to the disease.

He thought of Iona on occasions like today. In recognition

of its status as an official town, the leaders of Middleborough had thought it appropriate to build a larger meeting place. Leroy had never had much interest in the workings of town government but Charles had embraced a political role with a certain relish. Charles enjoyed politics, enjoyed the machinations and shifts, recognized the importance of gossip and innuendo, the formation of coalitions and the wariness of enemies. Most of all, Charles enjoyed power. Politics allowed him an opportunity both to acquire power and to assert power. Leroy had a certain distaste for his son's interest in such activities, a distaste that was offset by his begrudging admiration for his son's undeniable political skills.

The Lapham family was to be honored today for their donation of materials and labor in making the new town meeting place a reality. Iona would have liked this, he thought. The families arrived at the town center and assembled near the waiting town officials. Leroy was conducting a quick review of his grandsons when he realized that Charles was not with them. Charles then emerged from the back of the carriage. He had put on the jacket of his militia uniform along with his side sword. On top of his head was a full powdered wig as befit a leading English magistrate. He appeared quite satisfied with himself.

Leroy said nothing, unsure of what to make of his son's "statement". The ceremony went smoothly, words of acknowledgement and thanks. Charles accepted a proclamation from the town officials on behalf of the family and responded with all of the correct words of appreciation.

The families rode home in silence, Thomas driving the wagon, Arby in the back having retreated into his own unique world. Leroy's thoughts drifted in pleasant melancholy to the rhythmic cadence of the wagon, replaying the ceremony, a subconscious admiration for Charles' performance finding its way to his lips in the form of a tight smile. Again his thoughts returned to Iona. She would have been proud.

They had come from the same neighborhood in Leicester from similar social circumstances. Leroy was unique to the neighborhood in that he was an only child, son of Earl and Agnes. His father had been absent for much of his life, was known primarily for proficiency with his fists and for his steady patronage of pubs. The nights when Earl did return home were often unpleasant, filled with harsh words, in curse and in tone, with an occasional physical demonstration of frustration. Agnes suffered such abuse dutifully and with little complaint. She was an expert sewer and made fashionable clothing for a number of patrons. The fact that her income was steadier and more lucrative that anything that Earl was able to produce was a constant irritation to them both.

Leroy had once – just once, and only from his mother – heard reference to an older brother. No further explanation was ever offered. At a young age, before any ability to understand or articulate, Leroy knew that he was a special light in his mother's eye. She doted on her son and he responded in kind. This seemed to fuel a certain fury in his father that the young boy could never understand. He responded by retreating from his father, avoiding interaction and contact as much as possible. His father's ever-increasing absences made things easier.

He first saw Iona as he returned from delivering some

clothes for his mother. She was walking with her mother and two older sisters and he realized that they lived only a few blocks away. He was fifteen at the time and was soon to learn that she was thirteen. They shared the absence of a father – hers having died – and a love of dogs. He could close his eyes even now and see the teenage lovers romping through the local fields with their dogs. They married young and moved in with Agnes.

It took a while but their firstborn arrived after a difficult, laborious pregnancy. Leroy Junior quickly became known as "Arby", a nickname that stuck, deriving from a niece's difficulty in understanding that Leroy Junior was "our boy." It was soon apparent that Arby was different. Medical information about Arby's condition was sketchy and anecdotal. The teenage couple was advised that Arby was likely "not right", that his physical and mental development would be limited, and that they might want to have him "placed out" to a special home. Iona would have none of it, would entertain no such discussion, would react with an intensity that neither Leroy or Iona's mother had ever seen in her before, a fiercely protective flame of commitment. Leroy's response had been more muted but equally determined. He had had no grand expectations for his child, no illusions. He had of course hoped for physical health for both his child and his wife and had seen the peril and heartache that childbirth could entail. He only knew that his child would experience a paternal love that he had not, a love based on an uncompromising model that he had been fortunate enough to receive himself from his mother.

Arby proved to be a challenge, a trying, frustrating experience of dealing with his developmental difficulties. A "mongol" as his condition was politely called; an "idiot" as it was most commonly described. And yet the young couple wrapped him in a cocoon, a warm and special place, and Arby responded in kind. Much of his behavior seemed beyond his control and beyond their ability to intercede. But the challenge brought out inner resources in the couple, a geometric perseverance and commitment, and they were rewarded with a child who was filled with kindness, of a gentle spirit, an innocent purity.

Still, things were not easy with such a child. He was noticeable and much noticed. Slights and cruelties were begrudgingly accepted ... to a point. Iona proved to have an inner spring of maternal protection that could be tripped by undue hazing and ridicule. She proved to be quite a formidable catfighter. Many were the mothers who offered public ridicule and disdain for Arby only to learn the better that such thoughts should be offered outside of Iona's earshot. Leroy had inherited his father's fistic gifts and was quick to use them in defense of his son. It was soon public knowledge that comments about Arby would need to be physically defended.

Leroy's thoughts returned to the wagon ride home. He had one final musing about Iona, the recollection of the fight she had had with a fellow passenger on the voyage over, the children who should have been better controlled, the quick exchange of insults and the burst of fingers to the victim's face, a flurry of punches to the neck and throat, the poor woman in tears and bleeding from multiple scratches across her face. The victim's husband interceded just in time to face an infuriated Leroy who threatened to throw the man and each of his impolite children over the bow of the ship. It was a threat that he had fully intended to implement.

Thomas glanced up from the reins and caught the quizzical smile that was spread across his father's face. Leroy looked over, caught in his wanderings, but said nothing by way of explanation. He was proud of Thomas, so much like his mother, young and lean and strong and determined. Full of piss and spit. As Charles and Thomas had come along they quickly learned of the family code that comments about Arby were to be met by fists and fury. It was a lesson to which each quickly adapted.

They were approaching the sawmill now. The route to their home led slightly further down the road, less than half a mile. Charles had settled in off to the right of Leroy's property, angled out and away by about a mile. From the sawmill one could see chimney smoke from either house, something that Leroy valued and thought important. Leroy directed Thomas to stop at the mill and drop him off there. It was becoming late in the afternoon and Thomas protested that anything of business could wait until tomorrow. But Leroy was insistent on stopping and said that, after all of the day's activities, he would enjoy a slow walk home.

Leroy walked into the empty sawmill, alone in his thoughts, alone in the physical structure that he had built. The complex consisted of the main sawmill building, about thirty feet by thirty feet in dimension, that stood next to the waterfall. Against it was an addition of about the same size that served as a workshop for the craftsmen and storage area for lumber and tools. He was up to six employees now with two to three Nemaskets working for him at any given time. Next to the addition were a couple of smaller, stand-alone buildings used for miscellaneous storage. Finally, in the back was a fairly large area used by Thomas, his friend Edward Horton and other of their hunting partners, an area for skinning and drying, pelting and tanning of hides. The stench of the workings could be overpowering, particularly on hot, humid days, but Thomas loved his hunting and had created a lucrative trading business from it. Thomas primarily worked out of a small building made of stone that he kept locked up. He said this was necessary to protect his knives and guns. Leroy had noticed that only Charles and Edward had keys.

Leroy strolled from one building to the next, out to Thomas' hunting area, then circled back to the front opening of the sawmill, checking under lean-tos and stacking wood pieces that were askew. He became conscious of the mellifluous sound of tumbling water just outside the far door and realized that the waterwheel was still turning. He entered into the late afternoon sunlight, reached down and put the large peg into place that stopped the wheel's rotation. Leroy enjoyed the calming sounds of the waters spilling out and seeking their final level for the day. He took off his shoes and leggings then rolled up his pant legs and dangled his feet in the placid water. His face involuntarily scrunched as he braced for the icy first encounter.

How far things had come. He thought back to the day, so long ago now, at the nail factory where he worked, the foreman, a man named Billington, his face flushed and spewing profanity at him and two others. The machines had malfunctioned, the metal wiring had mis-threaded through the cutting mechanism, nails and fastener clips coming out off-center and misaligned. Hundreds of damaged product, a waste of materiel, the third time it had happened that day. Billington was understandably angry and took out his rage at those who had no choice but to be subject to his barrage. His screaming drew a crowd and the three press operators became the focus of his outrage, to the amusement of those more fortunate. Leroy had felt his face redden, then beads of sweat forming at his neckline and brow, running by his ears. The screaming became surreal, background noise, as he retreated inward in defense, into an inner shell. He thought of many things as he waited for the fury to subside. He was tired of being powerless, frustrated, like his father had been, of being the screamed at, at being the owner of no options. He sought release ... escape ... refuge. He had heard talk about new English settlements across the ocean and had always dismissed such thoughts as a lark. But now he thought differently, saw visions of green fields and open spaces, land without factories and smoke stacks and stale air. Land without machines and mechanisms. Land without cursing owners. Land without Billingtons.

As a final gesture, Billington took the metal pails from the front of each of the machines that had malfunctioned and flung their contents across the shop floor. Hundreds of properly formed nails went scattering in all directions.

"NOW PICK THEM UP!" he shouted.

Dutifully, the three men went to their hands and knees and began the arduous process of picking up the individual nails and putting them back into the pails. Billington watched for a moment, gave a final curse and was gone. The three men continued to pick up the nails, their physical position an accurate reflection of their social status. Finally, Leroy looked up and realized that the three of them were alone. Everyone else had gone back to their positions, their machines noisily re-engaged, the entertainment over.

That night he asked Iona to make the voyage.

CHAPTER 6

I t was always disconcerting to him, no matter how many times they had experienced such an encounter. Thomas and Edward proceeded cautiously into the empty village even as their dogs raced between the abandoned teepees. A *wetu* was what the natives called such structures. Teepees or wigwams as the English referred to them. In this case the settlement was relatively small, perhaps eight wetu at full build out. Five of the wetu were in various states of disarray and dilapidation, probably unoccupied for two full years. It was a tribute to their original constructors that the other three were in such good shape. They could see the skeleton frame of the wetu, young saplings that had been bent and stabilized, large structures, probably eight to ten feet across and just as high, the walls of tree bark still in place. The bear and deer skin covering of the dwellings were gone or decayed, frayed beyond recognition in most cases. But there were enough remnants for one to easily envision its prior inhabitants. That settlements such as this had been filled with vibrancy and live inhabitants only a short time ago had always spooked Thomas. They were a reminder of the particular vulnerability that the native population had when exposed to disease. And, clearly, the source of such diseases were non-native peoples.

They picked one of the relatively undamaged wetu, entered, and tossed their guns against the side walls. They swept away the covering of leaves from the center of the wetu exposing the blackened remains of earlier fires. Eerily, against one of the walls was a wooden crib that had once held this family's corn and succotash. A bow made from a sinewy maple sapling was next to it. Two wooden bowls could also be seen amongst the scatterings that were on the wetu's floor. It was only too easy to envision what ...

Edward tossed down his satchel and checked the corn crib. There were plenty of downed limbs and branches outside to make a fire and the crackle from the bright yellow-orange flame soon helped them forget where they were. They had seen many such villages, sometimes as few as three wetu, generally in a protected grove of trees or near to a small brook, always built the same. Occasionally they would find bones. To Thomas, the spirits of the previous occupants hung in the air almost as if smoke from a fire. He could never stop himself from wondering what had happened to them. Had they left, abandoning everything? Had they died in the spot where he was sitting, helpless against a force they had never before encountered, a force that they did not – could not – understand? Had their last thoughts been of bitterness or resignation? Had they watched their children die helplessly before them, listened to their leaders seek answers from the spirits? Answers that did not come?

Thomas' attention was snapped back to the present as all three of the dogs bolted into the wetu, full of excitement, butting into the side walls so that he and Edward worried about their collapse. Thomas brought his two dogs out into the open central area and began his familiar ritual. He tossed each dog a small stick and each dutifully fetched.

30

Again and again. Finally, he made a tossing motion causing both dogs to sprint after the imaginary stick. Each realized that it had not been thrown as he tauntingly held it up in the air, face-level, in front of him. As they raced towards him preparing their leap towards the stick, he picked out one of them and, timing his move perfectly, dropped the stick, grabbed a front paw, fell backwards to the ground to his seat, then onto his back all in one swift motion. At the same time, he lifted a bent leg and got his foot right on the stomach area of the dog and thrust outwards. The dog in question went soaring through the air, to Thomas' amusement and, apparently to the dog's as well based upon their persistence in repeating the activity.

As usual, today's hunt involved a search for bear and deer in order to bring in skins. They had not ventured far and had not planned on more than one night away. As the fire crackled Thomas looked across at the face of his friend, red-hued and wavy through the energy of the fire.

"We never find animals browsing in these deserted wetu. It's almost as if they know."

Edward shook his head and chuckled.

"Most of the time you just want to smash through things, straight ahead, head down. But we find one of these villages and you go all quiet, become a philosopher."

Thomas did not answer, just shook his head matter-of-factly, a subtle agreement.

"My mother asked me about you and my sister."

CHAPTER 7

L eroy was measuring a piece of lumber when he heard the familiar chanting sounds of Arby returning from his rounds. He thought nothing of it until one of his employees grabbed his shoulder and gently spun him towards the main opening of the building. In the distance, down the road, amidst a cream colored swirl of dust, he could see that Arby was sitting on top of his wheelbarrow, all excited and a-chatter, gesturing animatedly as he was being pushed forward by someone Leroy could not identify. They turned a bend in the path and headed towards the sawmill. To his astonishment Leroy could now see that Arby was being pushed by Attaquin, the local sachem of the Wompanoags.

Leroy knew Attaquin only by sight and by reputation. Attaquin was the oldest son of Pamontaquash, the elderly "pond sachem", and had increasingly assumed most of the responsibility for the day-to-day leadership of the Wompanoag people, including the Nemasket tribe. Most of what Leroy knew about Attaquin he had heard from John Sassamon. Sassamon had described Attaquin as a man of principle, a man truly concerned about the welfare of his people, and a man who dealt in realities, including the certain reality that coexistence with the English was the central point of change in the lives of his people. "A man that understands commerce," said Sassamon, in high praise. Leroy had seen Attaquin perhaps a handful of times and always from a distance, generally in a cluster of braves or tribal elders. Interestingly, Attaquin was known to bring his young daughter with him on many such occasions. Leroy had learned from Sassamon that the daughter was about eight years old.

Leroy had never felt the urge to meet Attaquin, never sought out any opportunity to introduce himself. There seemed to be no need. Two of Leroy's employees were members of the Nemasket tribe and they generally did all negotiating and purchasing of products on the tribe's behalf. Sassamon was always available for more complicated transactions. The tribe made great use of the buckets and planting tools that Leroy's operation produced and a number of the Nemaskets were skilled at making furniture, particularly chairs and shelving. Leroy had assumed that this was the way that Attaquin wanted things.

As they approached, Leroy could sense movement behind him and realized that two of his English employees had reached for their guns. Leroy shot them both a harsh look and held up a hand for them to stop.

Arby leaped from the wheelbarrow, his rusty hair all askew, his face flushed and engulfed in a toothy smile. He was chattering incoherently fast, so fast that even his father, with his trained ear, had trouble understanding any of his words.

"Attaqua! Attaqua! Weetompain! Weetompain!" Arby squealed incessantly.

33

The man-boy rushed to his father and threw both of his arms around his chest. Leroy responded in kind and said something low and soothing to him. They both held each other for a moment then Arby spun out of his father's grasp and turned sideways so that he could alternately address Attaquin and Leroy.

"Attaqua. Attaqua. Weetompain. Weetompain." he repeated, much calmer now.

One of the Nemasket employees came forward to try and serve as interpreter. Attaquin had observed the scene, expressionless, and now addressed his tribesman in a low, controlled voice. After a few minutes of conversation, the Nemasket interpreter turned towards Leroy and did his best to explain what had happened earlier in the day. It seemed that Arby had taken his normal route through the burial grounds on his way to meet his counterparts and pick up his cargo of lobsters. Unfortunately for Arby, the burial grounds were being used today and in a most special way. Arby had stumbled upon the funeral ritual being held for the last *"Wauchaunat"* in the tribe – the last member of the tribe that clearly remembered the time before the arrival of the English.

Metacom himself – known as Philip to the English - was in attendance. When Arby came along the path and saw the procession he immediately reacted with excitement and began his chanting and lurching movements. The first braves to notice Arby were members of Philip's contingent and soon Arby was surrounded by a dozen angry, menacing men. Attaquin had interceded and explained the unique arrangement that Arby had with the Nemasket tribe so Philip's men agreed to let Arby go. Fortunately, John Sassamon was attending the services and convinced Arby that he should return to his home without picking up his cargo. But Arby was reluctant and became difficult, noisy and disruptive, to the consternation of the large assembly. As Philip and more of his braves moved towards them, Sassamon began to fear for Arby's safety. Attaquin intervened again, said a few quick words to Philip, then gestured for Arby to sit on top of his wheelbarrow. Sassamon quickly completed the instructions and Arby climbed aboard. Attaquin grasped both handles, lifted with a grunt, and was on his way down the path back towards Middleborough. Arby had a new special friend, a "*weetompain*".

Leroy listened to the completion of the story and eyed Attaquin intently. Arby had returned to Leroy's side, an arm around his waist, his head nuzzled against the side of his father's chest. The excitement of the day's events was beginning to recede and Arby calmed considerably. Still, he continued to repeat, "Attaqua. Weetompain." in a subdued monotone voice. Attaquin stared back at Leroy, his dark brown eyes not leaving Leroy's gaze.

Attaquin seemed untroubled, his face serene, a striking looking man, wide prominent cheekbones, strength apparent in all his features. Leroy raised his hand, extending the index finger, a gesture for Attaquin to wait a moment. Arby released his grip and Leroy moved to the side wall of the building, pulled at a number of brand new buckets, finally selecting the largest one. Arby moved next to his father and both walked towards Attaquin. Leroy extended the bucket to Attaquin and the Nemasket employee spoke a couple of quick words about the gift.

Attaquin took the bucket in one hand and moved toward

35

Arby. The man-boy responded excitedly, his face brightening.

"Weetompain!" cried Arby.

Attaquin focused on Arby, his lips creasing into a smile.

"Weetompain," he said quietly.

Leroy moved over to his son who again grasped him by the waist. Leroy extended his hand to Attaquin.

"Weetompain," Leroy said firmly.

Attaquin hesitated for a moment then took Leroy's hand and eyed him directly.

To the shock of everyone, including his two tribesmen, Attaquin said in perfect English, "Thank you Mister Lapham."

With that, Attaquin turned and began his long walk home.

CHAPTER 8

He looked out over the placid waters of Assa-wompsett - "The Lake of White Stones" - directly into the late summer sun that was climbing above the opposite shore. A white smoky mist covered the lake, rising steamily above its dark waters, filtering the early morning sunlight that reflected off of the surface, drawn upwards, signaling the end of the night and the transition to a new day. "*Mautaubon*" they called it – the break of the day. Attaquin took off his moccasins and slowly headed towards the water of a small cove, through cool, wet mud, until his feet were covered. He loved this time of day, a time to be alone, before the day's activities distracted him from the simple enjoyment of still water. Simple time.

In truth, he had reason to feel so at peace. The harvest had been abundant, corns and squashes and gourds of all types. The banks of the lake were higher than normal and the fish stocks seemed especially plentiful. His tribe had settled in for the summer at the "Neck" region with its thick oaks and pines providing relief from the seasonal heat. Personally, he seemed to have overcome the effects of the debilitating illness that had struck him low the previous winter, the effects from which he could not seem to fully recover.

Attaquin could feel the morning's warmth begin to assert itself and with it, the subtle daily routines of the lake. He could see two fishermen on the shore some distance to his right, could see the wild ducks alight from the intrusion, two canoes further out headed to the middle of the lake.

His beloved daughter Tomisha was now eight years old, a sparkling and delightful child. He smiled to himself at the thought of her. At times like this he could not help thinking about his son, two harvests gone now, a victim of the ritual of manhood that Indian boys were required to endure. He could still see his youthful face, the last awkward smile, the quick embrace as he left him deep in the forests, armed with just the traditional hatchet, knife, and bow and arrow. He had been brave his friends insisted, had stood at close quarters with the bear, had endured the rapier cuts on his arms from the bear's parry. He had bled profusely but stoically. Eventually the arm swelled and turned a nasty purplish yellow, followed by the fever and the decline. Attaquin could still see the boys straggling into the village, the spring air cold but hopeful, the days lengthening, could sense an ill wind, eyes not returning his imploring look. He stood at the edge of the village, amongst the first trees, waiting. Waiting. Finally, the awful truth. The long, dull ache of yearning that would never heal. Sometimes Attaquin could hear his voice in a soft breeze, could see the sweet face, always a smile. If only he could have one moment, one word ... one embrace ...

Attaquin closed his eyes tightly, gulped, tried to clear the familiar stinging from the corners of his eyes. He tried to visualize pleasant thoughts, saw the smile, always the smile, took comfort in that clear memory.

His serenity was broken with the splashes of approaching feet, his brother Tokanauset. Younger than his brother and prone to easy agitation, Tokanauset nevertheless served his sachem loyally. Attaquin did not look over, continuing to stare out at the canoes becoming smaller in the distance.

"I am on my way to see Sassamon. Do you have any need of him?"

Attaquin shook his head absently, still reflecting.

"No. When is his next journey to Plymouth? Wish him a safe wind."

Tokanauset turned to leave but changed his mind. He admired his brother's leadership, his thoughtful ways with his people, the well planned tribal movements, the coordinated plantings, the systematic organization of the harvests. But he thought him a dreamer, an idealist. Nature afforded certain beauty such as what they both now beheld. But nature could also be harsh, requiring great strength and brutally unsympathetic to those who did not possess such strength ... or chose not to use it. Tokanauset was easily irritated by English activities, had voiced his concerns to his brother many times and had always felt dismissed. His brother favored accommodation. Adaptation. Commonality. Perseverance. The land was plentiful, he always said, the lakes and rivers stocked, the woods full. He insisted that the Wompanoags needed only to conduct an intelligent harvest. He argued that they could learn much from the English, already had – their tools, their buildings, their use of animals. The people – his people! – were better off adapting. Look how the English had made use of the Wompanoag farming techniques! His brother

Attaquin truly believed that a new society was emerging, a combination of two cultures that were on the verge of forming a new composite society, one different and more benevolent to both peoples. No, adaptability must be the way.

"What troubles you my brother?" Attaquin asked, still gazing at the far shoreline. Tokanauset seized the opportunity.

"What happens when the English settle on your cove and bring their houses and their animals and their fences down to this very shoreline? Where will Attaquin find his peace then?"

Attaquin wheeled around to face his brother, a painful look on his face, eyes scrunched, clearly annoyed.

"Not this again! Not now. *Mautaubon*, my brother. Enjoy the day!"

But Tokanauset had clearly struck a nerve and was not about to let up his assault. He allowed an appropriate moment to pass, disguising his real intent, encouraging his brother to presume that a calmness had returned between them.

"You know what I see when I look out across your lake?"

Attaquin stared at him blankly.

"I see poles! Rows and rows of fence posts! Sticking out of the water, all in a straight line, crissing and crossing, dividing up your precious lake into pieces, each one to be "owned"! Because that's what the English do – they "own". They will make their way down to your beloved cove and build and farm and herd and fence and when they are done doing that they will extend everything – everything! – out into this lake. Then they will teach their animals to swim and discipline them if they venture beyond their proper poles!"

Tokanauset paused now for breath and composure. He was sweating at the brow and had spittle at the corners of his mouth. Reflexively, he wiped his lips with his sleeve, all the while glaring at his brother.

"And then they will tell the Wompanoag to stay off their lake."

Both let the moment hold. Attaquin took a long, deep breath and turned away from his brother, back towards the far shoreline. Tokanauset stooped down to cup some water and splash it on his face. He was not through.

"The English are a reality", Attaquin began. "They are here to stay. There will be no more *"wauchaunats"*. What we need ..."

"You have become a dull arrowhead! You are in need of a flint! You deceive yourself AND your people with your thoughts of harmony! What harmony? English harmony, that's what harmony! Move along! Move along now. Relocate. This is ours now. They even have their "God" who tells them so! Eventually, you and our people and our animals and our plants and the fish and the birds and the woods will all meet at the same place – at the last English fence!"

Attaquin was stunned into silence by his brother's fury. Now was not the time for rebuttal. Tokanauset stormed away from the shoreline with one final retort.

"Some of us will fight!"

CHAPTER 9

C harles was at his desk negotiating with a customer when the first employee raced into the sawmill.

"There is heavy smoke coming from the south! Lots of it! Charles, it looks like it is near your house!"

The mill erupted in frenzy. Charles reached into his drawer, pulled out a pistol, and raced outside to his horse. He took off without escort in a mad dash down the road towards his house. There were six remaining employees, four English and two Nemaskets. Two of the employees gathered their arms and mounted their own horses then rode into the sandy dust in pursuit of Charles. The other four pulled a delivery wagon from the rear of the complex, threw a number of water buckets in the back, hitched a team of two horses and followed.

Charles spurred his horse on unsparingly and, in about ten minutes, he approached his home. He first saw his oldest son, Israel, running up the road followed closely by Rachel in a buggy with the other children. He could clearly see the front of the cabin and, surprisingly, it looked untouched. A cauldron of white-gray smoke was rising behind the house and soon it turned towards him, enveloping the house and threatening to overcome his panic-stricken family.

Charles leaped from his horse, placed his frightened son behind him on the saddle, and galloped up to the carriage. He could see that Rachel was distraught but in control.

"It's in the back, behind the house! The back corral and fence are on fire! The animals are ..."

Charles was off before she could complete the sentence. As he reached the front of the house, the smoke and acrid smell began to envelope him. He covered his mouth with a handkerchief and fought through the eye sting, making his way to the rear. He found the water trough, filled a bucket and blindly threw its contents ahead of him in a wide circular motion. The smoke receded a bit then immediately started back towards him. At this point the other two mounted employees arrived and all three of them continued to spray water into the smoke. As the other four employees arrived, Charles motioned them to take his place and he signaled for the two others to follow him. They made their way along the side of the corral fence, feeling their way through the smoke until they came to the source of the blaze. Next to the rear barn, where the two sides of the corral fence intersected, was a large pile of dry grass and hay that was raging upward in an angry orange-red ball. The smoke from the burning grass was swirling wildly first coming directly at them then alternatively swinging to the side giving them a clear view of the fire. Charles put his head down and charged the fire, ignored the singeing of his forearms and threw a bucket of water directly on the blaze. A torrent of white smoke came at him, blinding him momentarily with a noxious sting. The other two men also made their way forward and doused the fire with their buckets. Charles had recovered sufficiently to make his way back to the trough and begin the process again. As he turned towards the fire, he could see his two employees with their forearms against their eyes trying to grope their way backwards. He ran forward, dropped his bucket, and aided his two men back away from the smoke. The other four men had joined the fight and quickly brought the fire under control. As the smoke lifted away, the men could see the damage that had been done. It appeared that a pile of dried grasses and hay had been propped up at the corner of the fence along with a number of extra fence rails and the whole thing had been set ablaze. The fire had spread about four or five feet away from the corner and down the length of each of the fence rails leaving them charred and withered.

As the air cleared Charles could see that the gate to the corral fence had been opened. In the distance he could see some of his cows and goats meandering in various directions. His quick scan indicated that half were in sight and half were missing. Fortunately, there had been no damage done to his house, the main barn or the rear barn. He went into his house and brought out whatever food he could find for his men, some bread and pie and beer. After a few moments of refreshment, they all moved out into the fields and the woods to try and find the scattered animals.

CHAPTER 10

He first saw the dogs sprinting towards him and knew that Thomas was soon to arrive. Within seconds the first of the hunting party came into view. Thomas had been out for two days with Edward, three patrons from the Tamarack and three Nemaskets and, based upon the heavy trundles they were dragging, the trip appeared to have been productive. This trip was primarily for skins and Charles could see the piles of bear and deer hides. And, despite the coolness of the weather, the stench of the expedition preceded them.

The troupe arrived in the back area and began to dismantle. Thomas saw Charles standing by himself fifty feet away from the complex, dropped his gear, and walked around to the front side of the mill. As he neared his brother he broke into a huge smile, held his nose in ridicule of himself, and broke into a mock sweeping motion as if to brush away his scent. Charles remained stone-faced.

"We have a problem."

Charles paused to let his words sink in. Thomas realized that his brother was deadly serious.

"Yesterday there was a fire at my house. You weren't here, father wasn't here, I just reacted and rode to my house and everybody followed me." Charles lifted his head and did a quick scan to see if they were being watched. "So no one was here for probably an hour or so."

Thomas was sensing his brother's trepidation and had a sick feeling as to where the conversation was leading.

"After we put out the fire I told everyone to go home. I came back alone. When I got here I saw that the door to the stone barn was wide open. Someone had smashed the hinges and pried it open."

Before Thomas could get his question out, Charles responded.

"They're gone."

As Thomas felt the words sinking in they could see Leroy trudging towards them with his head down, pipe in hand. As he neared them his face contorted in response to Thomas' stench, half in jest, half involuntary reaction.

"Looks like you had a couple of good days."

"They were walking right up to us volunteering to be taken."

Leroy smiled in amusement, saying nothing. As the silence continued, the air turned unsettling.

"I had a Colonel Church come and see me the other day. Militia guy over in Taunton. Sassamon set it up. Said he

LOUIS GARAFALO

was interested in acquiring some of our new products."

Silence.

More silence.

Finally, Leroy cleared his throat and looked both of his sons in the eye.

"Boys, what exactly are you doing in that stone barn?"

The question hit them with a hammer-like force and they could feel the acid swirling in their stomachs, the sickening awareness that they both felt at their impending exposure. The confession that was moments away. In fact, they had kept their operation a secret, had felt it best to keep the information contained amongst themselves and Edward Horton, even to the exclusion of the man they admired.

Charles went first.

"We've been working with an iron foundry over in Taunton and that is where Colonel Church heard about things. Benjamin Church. I have actually met Colonel Church a couple of times, mostly at militia meetings. He's a good man. They have been making some pieces for us. We use them …"

Thomas broke in, "Father, we are making guns back there,"

Charles hung his head sheepishly for a second then lifted and began gently shaking it in agreement.

Leroy said nothing, contemplating the words, processing.

"Who knows about this?"

Thomas took the lead. "The three of us … and Edward."

Charles interjected. "That's not quite true. Sassamon and I have had some discussions …"

Thomas' face registered his shock and he shot his brother a look of disdain.

"There is some real opportunity here," Charles continued warily. "Thomas and Edward are the experts and have perfected the design and the specifications. We get the barrels and rods from Taunton and make the sights and final trigger pieces ourselves. The gunstock obviously …"

"I don't believe you told Sassamon! I thought …"

"Sassamon knew! Don't be naïve! He learns everything. … We do have Nemaskets working here you know." Charles cleared his throat, preparing to deliver the difficult news. "The day of the fire, everyone left to follow me. No one was here. I sent the fellows home and came back here alone and …"

"And?" Leroy intoned.

"… and I found that the stone barn had been broken into, the hinges had been smashed off."

"How much did you lose?"

"As best I can tell, ten new rifles."

49

Leroy nodded his head, absorbing the story, berated himself a bit for not having been more curious.

"So …?"

"I'm waiting for Sassamon to get back to me."

CHAPTER 11

B ased upon the three pewter mugs stacked in front of him he appeared to be drinking his fourth beer. John Sassamon had been warned as soon as he had approached the Tamarack that one Charles Lapham was looking to talk to him. And that Charles Lapham was a bit agitated. Sassamon had taken a deep breath, composed his thoughts, raised his head, and had proceeded through the front door. He had no doubt as to the nature of Charles Lapham's business.

Drinking did not become Charles Lapham. He rarely engaged in it and did not handle liquor particularly well. His father had been a strict teetotaler having seen the ravages that alcohol could inflict on a family. Nonetheless, Charles thought it appropriate to prepare for his conversation with Sassamon. Seated with Charles were four of his fellow militiamen.

As Sassamon entered the main pub area and saw the five men he instinctively shifted his mindset and his persona into a mode that had worked well for him in other such circumstances – he feigned blissful ignorance as to the purpose of Charles' need to speak to him. As he approached the table he maintained a tight-lipped smile and an expressionless look trying his best not to show any sense of intimidation. But there was no doubt about it – Charles Lapham was a big man.

"Charles, my friend," he stated calmly, extending his hand. "I heard about the unfortunate incident. Is there anything that I can do."

Charles was sweating profusely and was clearly distressed. For all his "preparation" he seemed to be at a loss for words, his mouth moving hesitantly but saying nothing. Finally his thoughts began to lurch forward.

"I want to know who is responsible," he said evenly.

Sassamon had also had plenty of time to anticipate the question and yet he too stumbled for an answer. In truth, he did not yet know who the culprits were. He had not tapped his normal sources for information nor had any information reached him voluntarily. As was happening with increasing regularity, John Sassamon was in a precarious position because of the unique span that he had into the two adjacent cultures. Anybody English assumed that he knew and was holding back information; anybody Indian assumed that he knew and had told those that were non-Indian. Sassamon's own personality had contributed to this perception. He enjoyed the role of intermediary, whether it be lingual, cultural, informational … or trafficking in gossip. He enjoyed his status as one who could exert influence or power over a situation and he made no attempt to minimize the perceptions of those who attributed great power to him. He was also not shy about seeking remuneration for his services. For Sassamon, compensation could take many forms. One of the most satisfying was merely his own perception that many others thought him to be a man of influence.

But life had become increasingly uncomfortable for the likes of John Sassamon. His early influence had come from his ability to communicate in both English and the various languages prevalent in southeastern Massachusetts. In his role as a "praying Indian" he had had the opportunity to work with mentors like John Elliot and others who were dedicated to spreading Christianity through communication in the native languages. Sassamon was quick to recognize that both the spread of Christianity - and the spread of commerce – were more fluid when one could communicate in both English and native tongues. And Sassamon was genuinely skilled in this role, quick in intellect and facile with language. This placed him at the top of a pyramid whose base was formed by the two primary populations. It gave him access. And influence. Status. And reward.

But the societies around him were changing and not to his advantage. Instead of a mixed society dominated by multi-cultural men like himself, the societies were increasingly in a tense standoff, fueled by conflicting motivations and ir-reconcilable visions. The flow of English settlers had con-tinued unabated, driven by a hunger for land and property, apparently immune to any native consideration. The native response of accommodation was seen by many to be insuf-ficient, impotent. Those in leadership positions within the native communities were particularly vulnerable as no amount of accommodation seemed to satisfy the insatiable English hunger for land. Worse, years of diseases had struck the southeastern Massachusetts area devastating the native population. The sense of comfort that had always come from numerical superiority had been replaced by a subtle yet desperate recognition that perhaps force, sheer blunt force, might be the only solution. Those that advocated force also preached urgency. Those that advocated for accommodation were losing credibility among their people. Many, like Sassamon, found themselves at the pinnacle of a pyramid - only the pyramid had been inverted. Those who were perceived to be part of the accommodation process became increasingly isolated, trusted by neither party, a source of wariness to both.

Sassamon was shaken from his idleness by a booming repeat.

"I want to know who is responsible!" Charles shouted.

Sassamon's adrenaline flowed now, aware of the tone of anger and hostility that surrounded him, a realization that Charles' frustration might become physical.

"Charles, I honestly do not know who was responsible. I am trying my best to find out. I have certain people who are trying to help me and I assure you I will let you know when I learn anything. Anything. I ..."

Sassamon heard his voice break, a nervous catch, and felt himself out of words, unable to speak. Recovery took a few seconds.

"Charles, logically speaking, I don't think you or your family were meant any harm. As I understand it, a pile of grass was placed at the corner of your fence and set afire. I think it was meant to rankle you, maybe even a prank ..."

"MY FAMILY WAS IN THE HOUSE! They could have been killed! I got there just as the smoke was turning towards the house! The fire would have turned next! Prank my ass!"

Charles chugged the last of his mug's contents and spilled venom at Sassamon, less than a foot away from his face now.

"WHAT IS WRONG WITH YOU PEOPLE? What is your problem? We come, we teach you to build, teach you about tools. WE TEACH YOU HOW TO OWN! Teach you about property! How to contain things and master things! What don't you people understand?"

The release of fury began to satisfy Charles a bit and he became more controlled.

"They burned my fence. I lost some of my animals. I want compensation," he leaned in closer to Sassamon, inches away now "and I want to know who did this."

"Charles ..."

"I want you to write a letter. Right now! To Attaquin ... or Tuspaquin. Write it to both".

Charles struggled for the right words, began a halting dictation. "You people ... no, your people ... burned my fence the other day causing distress to me and my family. And the loss of some of my animals. ... I demand a fair compensation. ... no, I demand compensation." His fingers twitched involuntarily as he pulled away from Sassamon, his mind searching for more words.

"What's your word for 'fence'."

55

Sassamon took some relief in their separation, beginning to feel that he had weathered the worst of the confrontation, a bit of confidence returning. He considered the question for a moment, his face forming the slightest hint of a sneer.

"We have no word for 'fence'.

Undeterred, Charles reached for the table and grabbed a mug, unaware that it was not his. He swilled heartily, put the mug down, and put both hands on the table, his back to Sassamon. A tense moment passed. Then Charles slowly wheeled back towards Sassamon, one eye cocked, a look of controlled fury on his face. In a voice close to a whisper he asked,

"How did you know there was a pile of grass at the fence?"

CHAPTER 12

As he approached his home he saw smoke swirling listlessly from the chimney. Strange he thought, Thomas had said he would be gone at least another day. Then he saw Charles's horse tied outside.

As he entered the house, Charles arose from a chair. In his hand he held a large black envelope. Leroy knew immediately.

"Father, it is about Grandma Agnes ..."

Leroy stood silently in the middle of the room staring at the envelope.

"I know what it is," he said quietly. He took the envelope from Charles' outstretched hand, moved across the room, and sat in his rocking chair.

"John Sassamon picked this up while in Plymouth yesterday. He wanted to come by personally to deliver it and to express his condolences. He came by the mill and gave it to me when you were not there."

Charles approached his father, unsure of what to do or say

next. Awkwardly, he attempted to give his father a hug by reaching down to him. His father did not respond. Leroy stared at the envelope, holding it at arms length, a hand grasping each corner.

"Do you want me to read it?

Leroy gently shook his head no. He got up from the chair and moved to the fireplace mantle. There, propped against the wall, was the pen-and-ink drawing, a portrait of herself, that she had had done and had given them as they waited to board the ship to New England. It all began to flow back to him now, her stiff, formal composure, the mindless small talk at the dock, the bustle of activity as the ship's crew made the final preparation, the call to board, her eyes filming over now, filling with tears, a hug for Iona and the children, a last desperate hug for her son, her blue eyes shining through liquid, a tight final smile, no words.

They all lined the deck to waive to her as the ship pulled out, her grandchildren excited and hoisting their hats at her, a lonely figure, fading now, shrinking in size and color. She raised her hand slowly, halfway up, her hand by her ear, then let it drop to her side. The children moved away from the deck, chasing a ball with some others. Iona draped her arm over her husband's shoulder then left him to his thoughts. He remained at the deck rail for another half hour, peering at the fading horizon, his life dividing.

That they would never see each other again was the great unspoken. The woman who had given him life and sustenance would have to be part of the price for escaping the Billingtons of the world. Neither he nor his mother could read. There had been a letter from her the first year and he had had Iona compose a response. They received one more from her six months later. That was their last correspondence.

Leroy took the drawing from the wall and returned to his chair. He took the frame and the black envelope and pressed them both against his chest. Then he rolled his head back, closed his eyes, and began rhythmically rocking, lost in thought.

He was oblivious to the sound of the front door latching.

CHAPTER 13

C harles saw them first, new immediately that something was terribly wrong. He was standing just outside the large opening of the mill directing the placement of some lumber pieces when he saw the group approaching, John Sassamon and two other individuals that he did not recognize. One was pushing the wheelbarrow while another was steadying Arby's body as it lay across the top. As they made the final turn in the path, Sassamon stopped the men in place and came forward to meet Charles.

"Something horrible has happened today, my friend. A terribly tragic accident."

He motioned for Charles to approach the wheelbarrow. As Charles neared the group he saw his brother's limp body, his head wrapped in a light colored garment through which much blood had seeped. Charles looked back towards the building and was about to suggest that the group leave the premise and head towards his own house down the road. But it was too late. Word had spread quickly through the building and all six of the workers present streamed out towards them. Next came Thomas and Edward who had been working in the back building. Finally, wiping his hands with a rag, came Leroy.

All moved aside to allow him to pass.

He approached deliberately, his face emotionless and stern. He moved directly to the body, addressing no one, and put a hand on the bloodied garment. After a few moments, Sassamon broke the tense silence.

"Mister Lapham, I am so sorry. A terrible accident has occurred today. ... I am so sorry for your loss, sir."

Leroy glared at Sassamon, glared through him, a torrent of emotions beginning their run through him, swirling, images and memories tossing about.

Then anger.

Then rage.

"Where?" Leroy spat out.

Sassamon took a deep breath, trying to brace himself for a fury that he felt may be imminent.

"It happened out on his normal path. Where the trail narrows, a slight embankment above the stream. ... It looks like he fell, lost his balance. ... They found his wheelbarrow in the stream as well."

Silence.

"Who is 'they'?" Leroy finally shot back, gulping.

Sassamon did not immediately volunteer an answer but felt his discomfort begin to dissipate as Leroy moved his attention back to his oldest son's body. He began to stroke the arms and shoulders, first with the front of his hands then with the back. He stooped low over the covered face and slowly, tenderly began to pull away the garment. The cloth stuck in spots where the blood had coagulated and he placed his hand at the back of Arby's head to gain some leverage.

It was then that he felt the huge lump.

The face now revealed, Leroy gently stroked the rusty hair and thickened cheeks, dabbed at patches of blood, retreating deep in his mind, trying to deal with the shock of his son's death and the disturbing evidence found on the back of his son's head. He felt strangely alone, thoughts of Iona fleeting into his consciousness, very clear now, images of the voyage over, building their first house, showing her the waterfall for the first time, Arby next to them holding her hand. More and more they came, overwhelming him as he closed his eyes and pushed his bearded cheeks against the childlike smoothness of his son's face.

Only Charles and Thomas remained, standing off to the side perhaps ten feet or so. Both looked at each other, stunned, as they witnessed something that neither had seen before in their lives.

Leroy Lapham was sobbing inconsolably as he clung to the head of his dead son.

CHAPTER 14

He was most a believer when he was preaching belief. On nights like this. On nights like this when he was in front of a room full of his people, their faces blurry in the flickering candlelight, faces that reflected back to him in deep golden tones from among the shadows, a rhythmic ambiance circulating through them, low undulations rising from the crowd, up to him, past him, through him, then pushed back through to them on the winds of his voice. He loved the preaching, the participation of the crowd, almost sensual in response to his message, a message full of words and cadence, tones and styles, uplifted spirits and mournful self-reflection. It all felt so natural to him, to lead and direct. To express to people and to move them.

He had had the finest educational preparation of anyone in the area, educated in Boston, at Harvard College no less, preaching in Natick, working with the estimable John Eliot in the translation of the English language into various native tongues. He was a man of formidable intellect, adept at structure and syntax. The native languages were consonant-strewn and difficult to the ear, full of lengthy words that often depicted complex situations or thoughts. The English language tended to itemize these complexities into simpler words, words that literally required a different use of the tongue. Breaking down the complexity of thought contained in a native word required that the thought be rebuilt using any of the multitude of English words available. Understanding differing meanings and subtle nuances was critical; order and inflection was critical.

Unquestionably, Sassamon had a gift for linguistics and he could move fluidly between the English language and the various native languages used throughout southeastern Massachusetts. This skill did not go unnoticed. Sassamon had often been used as the personal scribe of Metacom, or Philip as the English referred to him. To Sassamon's great satisfaction, many were aware of his special status.

Once, he actually believed. Or so he thought. Or so it seemed. Or maybe it was just his deep gratitude for the opportunity afforded him by John Eliot that compelled him to profess his acceptance of a faith that was the very catalyst for his learning. Maybe he was no longer a Christian but he continued to enjoy the preaching of Christianity. He enjoyed the uniqueness of its message – that a special man had once been among us – and the structuring of the sermon, the citing of passages and interpretation of their meaning, the translation into action and direction. The hunger of the audience for his words and the reactions that his words could engender.

But Sassamon was a practical man and a practical man could see that his skills were of most value in commerce. Commerce seemed to be the real religion of the English, the thing that concerned them day-to-day. As Sassamon had experienced them, the English were a people of growth and ownership and trade and accumulation. Such

activities required interactions and communications; nego-
tiation and agreement; transactions and documentation and
witness. Who better to provide such services? Who more
valuable?

The service was taking place in the new log cabin that the
Wampanoags had just built expressly for the purpose of
such gatherings, a concession that their *wetu* could not be
built large enough to accommodate them all. It was built
on the far shores of Assawompsett, set back perhaps a
hundred feet under a canopy of towering pines and oaks,
old growth whose stability attested to the many seasons
they had weathered.

The women had meticulously cleared the low scrub pines
and other brush from under the trees to form an open area
with a clear view of the lake. Already, a thick sprinkling of
pine needles had formed a natural carpet, soft to the foot
and comforting, soothing as a summer breeze. Sassamon
thought it the most beautiful spot he had seen in all his
travels and had plans to settle there himself. He often
thought of the old legend of Mon-do-min and the growth
of the first corn.

As the Wompanoag legend went, Mon-do-min was a
hunter who had become old and lame and could no longer
hunt. His wetu was located on the Nemasket River – "the
place of fish" as it was translated - and was situated far
away from the rest of his tribe. Mon-do-min had become
very weak from hunger and, one night, amidst a terrible
storm, had implored the Great Spirit to provide him food.
Shortly thereafter he heard the distressing calls of a par-
tridge that had flown into his wetu and gotten itself caught
in the wetu's poles and bindings. Mon-do-min gave thanks

for this gift and was preparing to roast the bird when he heard the anguished cries of a woman outside in the storm. Using all his strength, Mon-do-min went out into the driving rain and carried the woman back to his wetu, dressed her wounds, and laid her in a bed of bearskins. Having only enough food for one of them, Mon-do-min insisted that the woman eat. He told the woman that he took this encounter as a sign from the Great Spirit that it was time for him to die and travel to the Country of Souls. The next morning the woman found him dead and ran to tell the elders of the tribe. They chose to bury Mon-do-min on the banks of the river right where his wetu had stood.

That summer the Indians saw that Mon-do-min's grave was covered with a shiny green grass that had sprung higher and broader than any they had ever seen. Great green leaves emerged and, from them, huge growths of a special yellow grain. The voice of the Great Spirit was heard exulting the Wompanoag tribe about the sacrifice that Mon-do-min had made, that this grain was to be named after him, and that he was to forever be remembered for his kindness. The Great Spirit's gift to the Wompanoag was to be named "Mon-do-min" which, over time, had come to be more commonly known as maize.

Sassamon had often wondered if some other unknown Wompanoag had been equally noble and had been rewarded with the gift of trees.

As Sassamon continued his preaching he noticed Tokanauset standing against the wall next to the rear door. Sassamon continued on but had the distinct feeling that his message should become more succinct. Soon he had finished the service and moved to greet Tokanauset. Tokanauset held him by the arm until everyone had left the cabin then motioned for him to sit. He left for a minute then re-entered followed by five other braves. Behind them entered a stocky figure of medium height, powerful build, with a distinct, swarthy complexion and prominent facial features. It was Tuspaquin, the leader of the Nemasket tribe in Middleborough, known to both the English and the other Wompanoag tribes as "the black sachem". Sassamon knew Tuspaquin by another name – "father-in-law" – as he had married Tuspaquin's daughter Betty.

Tuspaquin greeted Sassamon cordially even though their recent acquaintances had been strained. Sassamon had always found Tuspaquin to be a complex man, multi-sided, amorphous. He was the sachem of a relatively small village but he had access to power via his marriage into the family of Massasoit. Metacom was one of Massasoit's three sons. Massasoit also had a daughter named Amie and she had married Tuspaquin.

While often guarded in his dealings with his father-in-law, Sassamon felt a kindred spirit with Tuspaquin. Both had dealt extensively with the English as Tuspaquin had negotiated a number of land sales with them. Yet, at the same time that he was a common trader with them, Tuspaquin also had a reputation of distaste for the English. Sassamon found no contradiction in this position, found this juxtaposition to be both logical and pragmatic. And, increasingly, his own.

"I am sorry about your friend Massa-ashaunt. I understand his services were most useful to you."

Tuspaquin stopped and looked completely around the

room, scanning for some unseen intruder. He leaned in towards Sassamon, a look of serious reserve on his face.

"Metacom has been having considerable discussion amongst the sachems. He has great concerns about the English. He has need of your services."

CHAPTER 15

I t had been two days since they buried Arby. The ceremony had been held at the First Church of the Green and Arby was laid to rest next to the thick trunk of an oak tree on the edge of the cemetery across the street. It had all been pleasant enough. Charles and Rachel took the lead for the family, coordinating the services, seeing to the appropriate aspects, making introductions. It was all properly done. As they filed out of the church to make their way across the street, Leroy had noticed that Sassamon and Attaquin were standing on the outer fringes of the crowd. He made a mental note to have Sassamon express his appreciation to Attaquin.

Leroy had found it all to be an ironic melancholy. The church was less than a mile from his house yet he was a stranger to it. Serious words were pronounced; words that Arby would not have understood and words that Leroy did not believe – words about salvation and redemption and God's will. Workers at the mill had taken Arby's wheelbarrow apart and used the wood as the basis of his coffin, an act of kindness that Leroy found incredibly touching.

As he had the day before, Leroy rode up to the gravesite, this time accompanied by Thomas. The autumn wind swirled gently through the thick trees, orange-brown leaves falling constantly. Leroy liked the spot very much, he thought the giant trunk and full boughs of the oak seemed protective, a continuation of what he had tried so hard to provide for Arby. He was not a man accustomed to sharing his introspections but Thomas noticed that his face masked a man deep in thought.

Thomas circled the grave, smoothing some of the dirt edges, removed some of the leaves that were rapidly collecting. He looked at his father and nodded. They were not a family given to displays of physical affection but he felt the strongest desire to put his arm around his father. He chose not to. Leroy bent down to one knee and smoothed some of the dirt himself, patting the ground gently. He rose to his feet, took a deep breath, and looked at his youngest son.

"Who'll deliver Sassamon's packages now?" he said softly, a mixture of sarcasm and whimsy.

Thomas looked at his father, his stomach unsettling, wondering if something else was coming.

"A dangerous business apparently," Leroy continued.

"You don't think he slipped, Father?"

Leroy contemplated the question, filled as it was with a sickening reality that he did not want to acknowledge ... or let go of. He thought for a moment about letting the question pass. Let Arby rest in peace, he thought. Let both of them have some peace.

He looked directly at Thomas, could see his serious face awaiting some unanticipated revelation.

"I guess it's easier to slip after someone has whacked you on the back of the head."

Thomas waited for more.

"I guess someone really wanted that box ..."

Thomas did not hear the rest of what his father said, the awful reality searing into him, the connection made, felt himself about to heave the contents of his stomach.

CHAPTER 16

He had felt agitated all day, a certain gnawing that he could not explain. The deaths of his mother and of Arby in the past weeks had weighed on him. He thought of them constantly. Such events cause a man to question his soul, to reassess his being. Leroy was not an introspective man by nature. He took no false solace in religion, could not bear its hypocrisy, saw its proponents as self-serving at best, generally misguided, and, at worst, people to be guarded against. His dogs were pure of heart … but his fellow men?

He thought it appropriate to treat men with respect … but only after a certain familiarity was attained, a confidence earned, after wariness was overcome. Only a fool could not realize the shortcomings of men, the ease of their temptation, the temporary nature of their belief. It did appear to Leroy that the Bible started off on the right foot i.e. that man had fallen. But his eyes and instincts told him that this was the natural state and no alleged savior had seemed to be able to change this condition over the past sixteen hundred years.

No, Leroy tended to see the world in terms of physical strength. Physical prowess. Those that had it, asserted it.

Those that did not have it aligned themselves with those that did. Life was a physical test in which men created their own rewards. In this regard he felt more connection to the native people, saw consistency in their beliefs in the one-ness of man with the natural elements. This made more sense to him, was closer to the world as he was experienc-ing it. Still ... still ... How to explain his love for Arby? His mother's love for him? Maybe there was another ex-planation, something in between.

The calendar had turned to late November and with it the graying of both the landscape and the senses. The bright colors of the foliage were gone now, their brilliant reds and yellows and oranges replaced by drabness, dull greens and faded browns. *"Taquonck"* – the fall of leaf – had ended; *"nanummatin"* – the winter winds from the north – were approaching. The time of year when a man naturally felt for his collar.

Leroy decided to take solace in the woods and streams that surrounded the mill. As the river moved past the mill and threw out its powerful torrents, it just as quickly settled back in to its natural flow. Only man could make a river hurry, Leroy had concluded. Water was a peaceful entity; only man could make it angry, and, even then, water al-ways returned to its inherent state – a purposeful yet unhur-ried meandering. Birds and animals and fish ... and Indians ... understood this. Below the mill, perhaps a half mile, the river turned and formed a small inlet, a shallow pond, and he had seen Nemaskets there fishing.

As was his wont, Leroy gathered two rifles along with his fishing gear and began to lumber along the embankment of the river. Within a few hundred yards, the embankment gradually fell off. The riverbed widened significantly, probably fifty yards across, with the water occupying only the middle twenty yards. On either side were scores of rocks, of all sizes, many smoothed down from years of water and wind. Perhaps a "*nanummatin*" from long ago had brought with it a rock storm along with rain, he thought. Leroy carefully picked his way along the uneven surface trying to maintain both his balance and his cumbersome load. He moved out into the middle of the bed walking just along the river, the grayish skies casting the slightest of shadows in front of him. Soon he was at the point where the bank turned and he could see the beginnings of the swampy wetland. Still further, the pond began to form, larger than he had remembered. Picking a spot amidst the wild reeds he tossed his rifles to the ground making a clattering noise. Voices from across the pond broke the silence. He was not alone.

Leroy stood up to surmise the situation and saw that two local Nemasket braves were across from him, maybe fifty yards away, apparently with the same intent that he had. He had expected that the braves would go back to their activity but such was not the case. One of them motioned to the other and both stared across the pond at Leroy. Leroy stared back, the situation taking on a strain, an unsettling air of discomfort. The braves began chattering to each other, soft at first then louder and louder, alternately looking across the pond at Leroy and back to each other. They were becoming more and more animated. Leroy continued to stare at their strange behavior, his eyes glancing down at the rifles at his feet.

Then, one of the braves began to chant in a loud monotone and began lurching his head forward, thrusting his hands forward as well, with occasional claps – an exact imitation of Arby. Leroy could feel the heat pulsing up through his chest, up into his neck, searing, the sides of his face flush, a gut twisting sensation from seeing this mockery. His primal instincts took over as be bent down to pick up one of the guns. It appeared that the braves, in their self-amusement, had momentarily forgotten Leroy's presence. In a frozen instant they saw Leroy's rifle leveled at them. Panic and the smash of the bullet arrived simultaneously for one of the braves as the boom from Leroy's rifle rang out across the pond and echoed through the woods. The brave inhaled a cry and dropped in a heap as the bullet smacked into his shoulder blade. The other brave turned to his right and be-gan running out of the tall reeds and back towards the river bed. Leroy picked up the other gun and ran to his left, also through reeds, until he reached the river bed and could see the brave trying to scramble up the slight embankment across the river opposite him. Leroy held his shot and raced over the flat stones, splashing through the shallow part of the river. He closed the distance on the fleeing brave who, back to him, was struggling with the slippery incline. Leroy stopped and calmly took his stance, measured the distance, readying to fire.

He never saw the third and fourth braves.

From behind him came a war cry and he instantly turned to the noise, saw the blurred body leaping at him, instinctively turned away to avoid the contact. The brave slammed into Leroy at shoulder level and bounced off to the ground. Leroy frantically tried to raise his rifle, desperate to fend off the other brave who was now on him. But it was too late. The fourth brave caught Leroy with a solid block to the body sending Leroy flying forward off-balance toward the edge of the river. He tried to right himself, the landscape swirling, instinctively swinging his gun in a wide thrust. One of the braves knocked him off his feet with a tackle around the knees. He heard the vague sound of a thud and his mind began to fog into gray. He heard only the sound of his own breathing, the sound akin to having his ears covered, and he sensed movement behind him. The second rock crashed into his head making a surreal sound, a long, distorted and extended moaning noise. He felt his face turn icy, aware of cold water seeping into his clothing, a dull, roaring pain, a changing of consciousness.

And then he saw her, straight ahead, her smile as bright as the summer day. She had a boat on a string and she was thrusting it out towards him, laughing, filled with happiness, beckoning him to grab it. He heard the inner sound of himself shouting gleefully to her, a five year old boy now, filled with childlike joy, felt himself reaching, arm and hand extended, reaching for the toy, a boy and his mother enjoying a last summer day.

CHAPTER 17

E dward Horton thought his friend had gone insane. He understood the stress he was under, the impact of the two sudden personal losses, the overwhelming grief. Certainly his distress could be rationalized. Still …

"I am pretty sure that I know the location they are preparing and I am also very sure that she will be there. We know the back approach …"

"You are talking about an eight year old kid! An innocent little girl! …"

"She won't be harmed Edward! She's bait, she's a bargaining chip. Nothing will happen to her. … I promise you."

"And then what? You really think he is going to fight you? Are you crazy?" Edward paused and they both let his words sink in.

"It may be more than Charles' stupid fence next time."

Thomas had anticipated all of it, knew that Edward was right, knew that Edward made sense, knew that this would be his reaction. And knew that ultimately he would be able to count on his help. The murder of Leroy Lapham was all that any of the English men in town were talking about and much of the discussion had been taking place at the Tamarack. Vengeful men, steeled by beer and numbers, were talking of action. Men who now realized the isolation in which many of them lived were ready to be pre-emptive. Edward himself had broached the subject of sending some sort of truce party to see Attaquin. He had been shouted down. Maybe send John Sassamon …. Shouted down. Edward saw clearly that demons were developing in this charged atmosphere, even among the most rational of the men. Rumors abounded that Tokanauset was recruiting a thousand braves from the southeast. That Sassamon had joined in the effort.

"My solution is the simplest, Edward. Think about it. Him and me. He's responsible for the actions of his people. He can't control his brother, we all know that. He's given Sassamon too much leeway. … We need to show them."

"Show them what? That we can kidnap a little girl? That we can piss him off by doing so? Attaquin is the only one we can talk to! He's normal! He understands things! Your plan is to make an enemy of the one Indian who we can actually deal with …"

"My plan is to eliminate the man who is leading a tribe of Indians that is out of control. To send the clearest damn message that any Englishman can send to the rest of them …"

"You just want vengeance."

"MY FATHER IS DEAD!"

Edward immediately regretted his words, sought to pull them back from the ether even as they left his tongue.

"Thomas, I'm sorry. ... I'll help you. I will. ... But can we talk this out a bit more?"

"What's to talk out? We kidnap the girl and that will require him to fight me. One of us wins. The girl is unharmed."

Edward's face went blank, his thoughts blurring, filled with conflicting emotions. Thomas gave him a moment.

"If he kills me then everything is fine. I'm at peace, so are you, and so is everybody else."

"What about Charles?"

"Charles thinks I'm out of my mind. He thinks Sassamon should solve this, find out who is responsible, convince Attaquin to give them up, hang them, move on."

"Why would Sassamon do that? He's a Wompanoag."

It was Thomas' turn to go quiet, to collect his thoughts.

"Because he's a businessman."

Edward went behind the Tamarack's bar and brought them both a mug of beer. Neither spoke for minutes. Edward broke the silence.

"When do we go?"

"Tomorrow afternoon. We'll leave at noon, trek the long approach and circle in from the rear, hide out at the old dugouts. The swamp is shallowest right at that point. As it gets dark we wait for an opportune time, sneak our way across, watch for what wetu she is in then go in and grab her."

"How are we going to get her back across?"

Thomas had to think a bit. "Make her swim, drag her ... I don't know. But once we have her we'll figure that out."

Edward could see that his friend was deadly serious, the momentum of the plan irreversible.

"Can I make a suggestion?"

Thomas lifted his eyes in response, awaiting his friend's answer.

"The women generally are up early to get water. We know where the spring is. We get ourselves across early and surprise them. Hopefully she is with the women helping them. If not, we wait. Watch for an opportunity."

"You're talking about crossing the swamp in the dark?"

"It will be the toughest way to cross but it's got some advantages. One, we're in total darkness but can use the light from their fires to help us find our way. Two, most, maybe all of them, are asleep. Three, we can keep our guns out of the water easily without being seen ... we may end up needing them."

Thomas looked away, processing the plan.

"That means we need to leave soon."

Edward raised his mug towards Thomas awaiting his friend's response.

"Drink up."

CHAPTER 18

They were wet and cold, having trekked for nearly five hours in the spitting rain, an angry dark sky and a low, incessant wind being their constant companions. They could have shouted and aroused no attention. Fortunately, a bright full moon provided some guidance for them as it flicked in and out of rapidly passing clouds. They moved in silence, slicing their way slowly through the marshy interior, could tell by the viscous mud that they were getting closer. The dark shadows in front of them thickened indicating tree growth and they felt the ground incline ever so slightly. As Thomas led them through the thick brush and low scruffy pines he literally bumped into the first of the abandoned wetu. There were four others, all in equally dilapidated shape, half of the siding broke or bent to the ground. They would provide no cover for them.

"The dugout is over here," shouted Thomas and be quickly veered off to their right. Edward followed, head down. Situations like these always made Edward marvel at his friend's comfort out in the elements, his inherent sense of direction and topography; his ability to locate. It made Thomas an excellent scout, tracker … hunter. The dugout was a wooden lean-to, still in rather decent shape after some years of abandonment, which had been used by the Indians as a storage area and corn crib. A side wall and part of the roof were still intact providing at least a corner of protection from the elements. They set their rifles and satchels down and both began pulling parts of the wetu across the small open area. They were quickly able to construct a partial wall of protection and expand the space so that both could sit against the back wall of the lean-to. The ground around them was moist, soft and spongy, with a smell of decayed wood.

Edward pulled his knees to his chest, tilted his hat down over his head and leaned back against the wall. Thomas was fidgety, alternately trying to strike the same pose then bolting upright to look up at the moon and passing clouds. Thomas estimated a few more hours before daybreak. Neither spoke.

Thomas reached into one of the satchels and found the loaf of bread and the crab apples that Edward had scrounged from the Tamarack's kitchen. He broke the bread in half and was met by Edward's extended hand. He clearly was not asleep. Edward tilted his hat upward, leaned forward a bit and they both ate ravenously.

"We don't have to do this you know," Edward stated matter-of-factly, without a hint of challenge.

Thomas thought on the words for a moment, a surge of appreciation for his friend moving through him.

"I know," he said softly.

Edward turned towards him and looked him straight in the eye.

"We can still grab her," he said. "It does not mean that there has to be some duel or fight or anything. This will certainly show your anger and your desire for justice … but it doesn't close the door on any other alternatives."

"I know," replied Thomas, his resolve stiffening and his mind engaging on the task at hand. "Let's get ready."

The two men rose and began checking their rifles. Each had brought two. In one of the satchels they had placed dry powder, well protected by some extra clothes, plus extra bullets and two hand pistols. They had also brought two small pieces of rope and two small handkerchiefs. They decided to take only the binding material with them as well as all four of the rifles. Thomas figured that they were perhaps a hundred yards from the edge of the swamp. As they moved stealthily through the thick entanglement of tree and brush, Edward stumbled over a small log. He grabbed Thomas' elbow and motioned for him to pick up one of the ends as he lifted the other.

After about fifteen minutes they were approaching the swamp's edge. As the clouds moved past the moon they could see bits of the dark open water that they would have to cross. Thomas had guessed it to be five feet at its deepest but could not really be sure. Edward's idea was for them to float the log along side them and balance their guns and satchel on it. They were within five yards of the edge now, could look across and see flickering embers from two fires. There can't be many of them, they thought.

On the far horizon they could see the earliest beginnings of the new day. They eased themselves ever so gently through the last edges of brush, the mud gushing through their shoes, soon replaced by cold, dank water. They emerged through the last of the bush, fully exposed now, and pushed the log out into the open water. They looked at each other both thinking the same thought – there is no easy way to do this. Thomas went first, bent low, moving quietly but steadily into the freezing water.

He felt his pant legs absorb the initial shock, felt the icy sensation working up to his thighs, to his belt line, tried to ignore the jolting shock by keeping his focus ahead to the physical location across the way and to the task at hand. Behind him he heard Edward let out a low, hissing cry as he too entered the frigid swamp. They were quickly in belt high water. They balanced the rifle and the satchel on the log, leaned forward into the water, their knees bent, more shock as their shirts absorbed the swamp, waited for a moment to regain control of themselves. The rain had stopped but the wind still whipped at a substantial clip and they could see saplings and low pines swaying in response.

They started across.

It took about ten minutes for them to reach the other side, the route being surprisingly unencumbered other than avoiding various dead tree stumps. They could see the morning going through its initial brightening, the dark purple of the sky beginning to lighten. Their timing had been perfect. They heard the low gurgling sounds of the spring and soon found the water source. To the right of the spring along the edge of the swamp there was a very large wild bush that seemed to be growing out of a fallen tree. This provided excellent close-in camouflage. Unfortunately, at that very point, the swamp edge dropped off sharply. At that spot they would be very close but they would have to overcome the difficulty of quickly getting out of relatively deep water and up a small embankment. To the left of the spring was a spread of swamp grasses maybe a foot high that ran all the way down to the shoreline. It would be easy to sprint up this grassy patch, perhaps ten feet, but there would be no initial camouflage from which to spring. They huddled under the protection of the wild bush, crouching low in the water, only their heads exposed.

"You stay here," Thomas commanded in a whisper. "I am going to go over to the left near the grasses and see if I can find any protection. Give me one of the guns." Edward delicately lifted one of the rifles from the log. "Put the other three up here."

Thomas paused and peered forward. "Let me go first. I'll come out of the water directly at them and grab the girl."

"IF she is here," Edward interjected.

"If she is here," Thomas confirmed. "If she is here, I am going right for the girl. I need you to take care of the others. When I make my move, go up behind the group to cut off their escape backwards. If it is a bunch of women we should be all right. If there are a bunch of braves then .... "

"Then we have four shots," Edward replied assertively. "Let me fire first. All three. Concentrate on the girl. Save your shot for last."

Thomas raised his gun with one hand and grabbed his friend's shoulder with the other. "If she is not here then we just lay low, wait and go home. ... If this gets rough then I want you ... I demand you ... get the hell out of here back across the swamp." His eyes were wide and fluid. "This was my idea ..."

Edward met his stare, gave him a reassuring smile, then dropped his eyes and went to work placing the guns on the embankment under the bush.

Thomas waded to his left a few steps, about to cross in front of the spring area, then halted and moved back to Edward.

"Let me have this," he said, taking the log. With that he moved across the open water, pushing the log ahead of him, and stopped in front of the shallow grassy area. He was probably twenty yards away from Edward. The swamp water was a dirty brackish green with a soupy yellow film on the surface and was only about a foot deep. Thomas moved to the shore and put his gun into the grass which quickly swallowed it from sight. He picked two large clumps of grass and spread them gingerly over his hair. It seemed to effectively cover his head and he could see through the hanging grass blades. Careful not to disturb his head covering, he made his way three feet out into the water and back to the log. Ever so carefully he laid himself down onto the swamp bed and thankfully felt his backside submerge. He positioned himself behind the log, adjusted two blades of grass, and listened to the sound of his shallow breathing bouncing off the swamp surface that was inches from his face.

Even as his body was shivering, Thomas dared not move. He was aware of the incredible sensation of sound and motion and rhythm that was the natural order of the swamp. He felt the sense of discovery that was being made of him by various insects and creatures, welcoming an intruder. This concentration actually helped him stay focused and alert.

All sense of time seemed lost to Thomas as the sky continued to brighten. His eyes stung and felt incredibly raw and his neck seemed stiffened into a fixed position.

Then, he heard the first voices.

His senses leaped to attention, fueled by adrenaline, oblivious now to his watery discomfort. He heard the voices come closer, could not make out how many. He looked to his right but could see nothing of Edward, could only hope that he was engaged. He heard sounds that appeared to be someone running, had all he could do to keep himself in his prone position, the moment imminent.

Then he saw her.

She was a striking little girl, petite, black hair pulled back, wearing a long deerskin dress and a red necklace, probably beaded cranberries. She was carrying a fairly large water bucket and appeared quite out of breath and quite happy about something. Perhaps the winner of a footrace? She turned back and had excited words for someone yet to come into view. Finally, an elderly lady arrived, a grandmother type judging from her appearance and stature, carrying a smaller bucket. They exchanged words and laughed as both bent down to collect water from the spring.

Thomas paused for a few more seconds to see if any others were following them. No one else came into view and he realized that his moment had come. For a split second he found himself unable to move, stuck in an incredulous inertia, a surreal dimension. Then, as if observing himself as an external other, he felt his body lift out of the water, raise to full height and begin a mad sprint up the grassy stretch towards the two figures. The elderly women looked up first, her eyes drawn to the movement at her periphery. As she saw Thomas racing towards them, her face instantly transformed into a mask of fear, uncomprehending, as if she had seen an apparition ... or a monster from the sea. She could make no sound, only stare blankly, open-mouthed as he rushed forward.

The girl turned her head towards him in response to her elderly companion. Likewise, her reaction was one of disbelief and Thomas could see her body visibly tense up with fear. To his immense relief he now saw Edward circling behind the two women, unseen by either of them. His hand cupped the mouth of the elderly woman and he quickly had a handkerchief gag over her lips. Seconds later her hands were tied behind her and Edward had forced her to the ground. Thomas was on the girl now and used the wet handkerchief he had in his pocket to gag the girl's mouth. Their eyes met as he did so and he could see that she was consumed with fright, in complete disbelief, her eyes wide, black and liquid. Edward was next to him now scanning back towards the encampment from which the women had come. He held the girl's arms as Thomas tied her hands and feet. Thomas and Edward looked at each other. They were done. It had all gone incredibly smoothly.

Edward helped Thomas hoist the little girl horizontally over his head. Then he gathered the satchels and all four of their rifles and began wading into the swamp. Thomas shifted the girl over his head, balanced his load, then also proceeded to plow through the swamp. Thomas could focus on nothing except crossing the expanse ahead of him. He could hear his own heavy breathing and could feel his arms leaden from the weight. He dared not stop, keeping his forward momentum at any cost. From the corner of his eye he could see Edward pirouette a couple of times looking back to see if they had been noticed yet. His face had a look of grim determination and indicated no exposure to danger. As the water got shallower Thomas shifted the girl from overhead down across his shoulder as if carrying a musket. He reached the embankment first, overcome with an incredible sense of relief, made his way through four or five yards of underbrush and finally set the girl down on the ground. Edward was just behind him now scrambling through the dense growth. He stopped next to Thomas, exploding exhales, and silently began shaking his head as if acknowledging the wonder of what they had just achieved. Edward dropped his load and lifted the girl over his shoulder. Thomas, welcoming the switch, picked up the guns and satchel. Across the swamp they could hear the first wails becoming louder.

CHAPTER 19

The swirl of events was beginning to overwhelm Attaquin. Two local Englishmen from the same family had been killed within a month's time and both under mysterious circumstances. The elders were advising that he move the women and children into the great swamp area as a precaution and were awaiting his decision. Attaquin was desperate to talk to John Sassamon to get his assessment but his braves seemed unable to locate him. Tokanauset had not been seen for two days and Attaquin feared that he might be seeking help from the Pocassets or the Narragansetts. Maybe from Metacom directly. Attaquin would take whatever measures necessary to diffuse the situation but was unsure who to talk to or even if he would be received. Perhaps he should just journey to the Lapham mill by himself, unarmed, and seek out Charles and Thomas Lapham on their ground, a demonstration of both his courage and his will to ease the tensions.

Where was Sassamon?

Attaquin had asked to be alone, believed a solution would come to him. He moved towards the central fire of the wetu and saw the shadows that were being cast on the far wall. How ironic he thought, dark and fleeting shadows cast amidst such a beautiful golden hue. He thought of Assawompsett, its beauty, its serenity, thought of his discussion with Tokanauset, his perception of things so different. Perhaps he should just invite the Laphams to come with him to Assawompsett some early morning, watch the rise of the sun – *mautaubon* – and the beauty of the breaking day. Certainly, there could be a peaceful resolution.

His thoughts were interrupted by the rustling of the bearskin covering. One of his elder braves entered, a look of despair and trepidation on his face. Attaquin greeted him with silence. What now? What else?

The brave was clearly uncomfortable, silent for too long. Attaquin raised his hand and stretched out his fingers, a gesture for the man to speak.

"Attaquin, Tomisha has been taken."

Attaquin heard the words, uncomprehending. The brave looked stricken and again tried to explain that Tomisha had been taken by some Englishmen. Attaquin leaped to his feet, his mind swirling from the sickening news. His reactions were interrupted by the entrance of John Sassamon into the wetu. Sassamon's face looked ashen.

"The Laphams have taken Tomisha. I am assured that she is safe and will not be harmed. The younger Lapham blames you for the death of his father and brother. He wants a duel."

CHAPTER 20

They rode in absolute silence. He had stayed the night at Charles' house and Edward had arrived early to pick him up. Charles had arranged for a number of the militia to accompany them to the duel site and now, as they headed into town, the wagon was surrounded by Charles and six of his men. Their guns showed prominently.

He had slept fitfully and his stinging eyes begged for relief. He glanced at Edward and then back at Tomisha who was sitting quietly in the back seat. She had been told very little, only that she was going to be released and that they were taking her to see her father. Thomas' body was already full of adrenaline, his senses at a new level of alert. He had hunted his whole life and had experienced the sensation of wild animals rushing him. But those situations had always been reactionary. This time he had the burden of time and apprehension, of anticipatory fear.

The duel was to take place at nine o'clock at the open field next to the land of Samuel Pratt. John Sassamon had picked the spot, a naturally open area, slightly rocky and surrounded by trees. It was about an equal distance away for both Thomas and Attaquin to travel. Sassamon had negotiated the terms under which the duel would be held – a knife and a tomahawk for both men. Only ten observers from each side, no weapons allowed for any observer. Tomisha to be returned unharmed. No other rules. A fight to the death. Francis Coombs, an elected Middleborough official, and Sassamon would supply the weapons and handle the logistics.

Word of the kidnapping and subsequent duel had leaped through the English and Indian populations causing considerable apprehension amongst both communities. The deaths of Arby and Leroy Lapham had generated much discussion, discussion that filtered through a different prism depending upon the community. Arby's death was still viewed as an accident by the Indian population and Leroy's death, while clearly a killing, was considered to be the unfortunate result of his own over-reaction to a perceived insult. As it was, he had seriously injured one Indian in the shooting and clearly would have killed another Indian had he not been forcibly restrained. The English community reverberated with the belief that Arby may have been murdered in the course of a robbery and that Leroy was killed in the course of justifiably defending his family. The Indian community continually pointed out that the robber or robbers had not been caught and could not be assumed to be Indian. The division within the communities – and the stalemate of opinion – would continue until the kidnapping of Tomisha by Thomas clearly escalated the stakes for both sides.

The wagon and entourage rolled forward, almost there now, and, from his mount, Charles could see a group of officials already in the middle of the field. Sassamon was clearly visible talking to Francis Coombs. Edward brought the wagon to a halt and instinctively moved around the horses to help Thomas dismount. Thomas had already stepped down and was moving his arms and shoulders in a swirling, loosening motion. Edward stopped in front of his friend who looked past him as if distracted – or concentrating – on the center of the field. Finally, Thomas reacted to Edward's presence and stopped his movement. His mouth was tightly pursed and he had a steady, unblinking stare about him. His eyes caught Edward's and Thomas gave him the slightest of smiles, a tight little upturn, a gesture of confidence ... or resignation. Edward sensed from his friend a kind of acceptance, a recognition of a force that could not be turned, a moment pre-ordained. Thomas cleared his throat and spit, nervous energy flowing through him again, moving him involuntarily.

Charles wheeled his horse over in front of his brother and peered, expressionless, into his face. His lips were moving and pursing as if trying to loosen something from the inside of his mouth. Finally, unable to express his inner thought, he reached down and placed his hand on Thomas' head. Thomas reached up and grabbed Charles by the forearm, found Charles' eyes and nodded affirmatively to him. Both could hear the commotion from across the field – Attaquin had arrived.

Edward went to the back of the wagon, untied Tomisha and led her by the arm to the edge of the field. Surprisingly, she did not leave Edward's side, did not move to escape, was a bit unsure of just what was happening. From the woody area on the far side, Attaquin stepped out into the field, clearly visible now to his daughter. Tomisha gave a slight cry and began running across the field. All movement stopped and all eyes were directed towards the little girl, in full sprint, past Sassamon and Coombs who swiveled to

95

watch her as she raced by. She never slowed down. Her back to the Englishmen, she approached her father, who had bent to one knee, and leaped into his outstretched arms. They locked in embrace, Tomisha's arms in full clutch around her father's neck and shoulders. Attaquin rose to his feet, lifting her in the air with him, said some inaudible words to her, and swung her gently from side to side. After a few moments and a few more words he let her slide down his body to her feet. Then he gestured for her to go into the woods and join with his braves. He followed her movements the entire way until she was hand-in-hand with one of the braves, and, only then, did he turn towards Sassamon and Coombs and begin to walk to the center of the field.

Thomas let go of his brother's arm, a final look, caught Edward's eye, another tight smile and began a quick, deliberate march towards the men.

As they approached Coombs and Sassamon, both men could read the face of the other, each thinking thoughts untrue about the other, each stalking a phantom, both faces a mask of determination. The faces of men about to encounter a dangerous unknown. Coombs held open a box containing two identical knives and two identical tomahawks as Sassamon began issuing instructions. Despite the cold temperatures, Thomas realized that Attaquin was shirtless and he too removed his shirt. Both men cut striking appearances, both in different ways. Attaquin had the mature strength of a thirty year old, stouter, cinnamon colored skin, jet black hair. Thomas was taller, leaner, starkly pale, wild brown hair.

In a loud voice, Sassamon spoke further instructions to the crowd, words that neither Attaquin nor Thomas heard, their minds retreating into a soundless void, energy beginning to rush up the middle of their bodies, all functions deferring to the challenge at hand. Sassamon spoke his final words, paused for one last moment, nodded to both participants, and then he and Coombs began to leave the field. Attaquin and Thomas both watched them leaving then turned towards each other, almost unsure of what to do next or how to start. Finally, from the edge of the woods came an ear-splitting sound, a combination screech and squeal, as To-kanauset screamed out a war cry. With that the two men sprung into action beginning to circle each other.

From an aerial view the scene below would have appeared orderly and symmetric, a square brownish patch of ground surrounded by the dull green and brown colors of the winter woods. All framed against a cloudy, steel gray sky. A row of stick figures, static, unmoving, standing directly across from each, the two participants in circular rotation in the middle of the field. All so quietly geometric.

But on the ground a certain ferocity was occurring, a fury bursting forth from both participants, both fueled by the vision of grievous wrongs having been done to them, both representing more than themselves, finding reserves within themselves that most men never tap. Or even know exist.

For perhaps ten minutes it went, Attaquin slashing first, aggressive and powerful, spewing unintelligible words at Thomas, his mind a-race at the transgression against his daughter. Thomas countered the moves, quicker, but defensive, in laser focus at the movements of Attaquin's hands. Attaquin thrust his knife once, twice, a third and fourth time then swung his hatchet viciously at Thomas. Thomas struggled to retain his balance, sidestepping, then backpedaling away from the fury. Attaquin rushed him and Thomas surprised him by planting a back foot and slamming the hatchet against Attaquin's forearm. Fortunately for Attaquin, the blade had turned sideways so the blow barely cut him. Still, the first blood of the fight had spilled. Attaquin reacted with even more energy, the sight of his own blood infuriating him, a source of renewed incentive. He shrugged his shoulders and hips, feinting at Thomas, then sprang forward in a charge. Thomas was able to evade the thrust by shifting to his right but not until their arms and shoulders had collided. Both swung their weapons wildly, each nicking the other. Thomas began to bleed profusely from his shoulder and down his bicep. Attaquin now had bleeding slashes on both forearms. As each continued to thrust and parry their blood began to spray so that both became spotted with patches of red.

They continued to assault each other, stalking, thrusting, the air filled with grunts of exertion and screams of profanity, each hammering at the other's arms and hands, nicking the other with their blades. Both were feeling the exhaustion, inhaling deeply, struggling to find resources of energy and nerve. At last, Thomas had a breakthrough. Attaquin had continued to aggressively pursue Thomas and, after a number of consecutive thrusts, Thomas was able to time his response and strike Attaquin full on the wrist with the head of his tomahawk knocking Attaquin's knife from his hands. Attaquin responded quickly. Thomas' momentum had continued his own arm movement forward and Attaquin was able to get a full grasp on Thomas' forearm. Attaquin tried to steady his hold on Thomas while thrusting his tomahawk towards Thomas' chest. Instinctively, Thomas spun backwards and away from the thrust all the while shaking his arm trying desperately to free himself from Attaquin's hold. Fortunately for Thomas, the blood and sweat of both men were smearing Thomas' arm forming a slippery solution that caused Attaquin to lose his grip. But the spinning efforts caused Thomas to lose his balance and stumble. Attaquin leaped in pursuit, continuing his attack, sensing an advantage, a turning of momentum. He let out a primal yell, reaching for reserves from the deepest part of his being, a culmination of effort that he sensed would lead to finality. Thomas was in full retreat, backpedaling, trying desperately to recover his balance. Attaquin swung frantically with a cocked fist, missing, but followed it with a solid punch to Thomas' neck and shoulders that sent Thomas reeling once more. The punch had caused Thomas to drop his knife and instinctively he began to bend to retrieve it. Attaquin seized this opportunity, let out a bellowing yell and charged Thomas full bore. Caught in a compromised position, Thomas awaited the blow.

And then, instantly, stunningly, everything changed.

From somewhere deep in his mind Thomas reacted as he had so many times before. He felt himself reach out for Attaquin's arms, allowed himself to go limp in preparation to absorb the force, lifted his knee and foot and was able to get it firmly planted at Attaquin's waistline. As his back hit the ground, and with an effort that he had never before used, he pushed Attaquin's body up and over him, getting Attaquin airborne.

Attaquin landed on his face and chest with a resounding, and ominous, thud.

In sheer reaction mode, fueled by a last injection of adrenaline, Thomas seized his opportunity. He brought the head

of his tomahawk down forcefully, barely missing Attaquin's head but hitting him full in the shoulder blades. Attaquin let out an audible gasp and tried desperately to crawl
forward, away from danger, his hands spreading before him
in an effort to rise.

The second blow caught him flush on the side of his head.

As did the third.

Thomas was completely spent, had to halt his assault, the
rapid, repeated swings having sapped his remaining energy.
He could see that Attaquin was immobilized, sprawled, his
limbs moving on instinct. As Thomas prepared to begin
swinging again he stopped. Blood was now streaming from
the side of Attaquin's head down his neck and through his
ear. He was no longer moving. Something deep inside
Thomas told him to stop.

Attaquin's thoughts began to turn gray, his body at peace
and one with the ground. He felt a light breeze push against
his face, a pleasant, soothing sensation. The wind picked up
now, swirling beneath his arms and his neck, lifting upwards until it seemed to be under his whole body. He felt a
calming relief, felt himself in a transition, the air swirling
and the wind still lifting up, gently at first then quicker. He
felt himself rising, a sweet, gentle sensation, felt his body
release, lightening his spirit, rising upwards above the field,
a cross current of breezes mixing in, cooling him, soothing
him, balmy, an untold peace overcoming him, carrying him
into the currents. Higher. Away.

Away ...

Thomas fell to his knees, beyond exhausted, his senses beginning to recover, his mind allowing the blotted sounds to return to his consciousness, could hear Edward now, and Charles, their voices distant and tinny, beginning to phase in more clearly, louder but still unintelligible, his mind honing, returning from a most demonic place. He could take no joy in his victory yet, could think of nothing but getting to his feet, still in fight mode, as if visualizing Attaquin's return in a different format.

As his senses sharpened, he felt the field return to color, the air return to coolness, the voices and noises return to proper volume. He could hear Charles and Edward now, felt their backslaps, could not react to them. They began leading him away, their voices again fading to white noise as his mind retreated for a final time to that awful place that it had just been. He could only blink and stare straight ahead as they led him away.

Behind him he could hear the wails as Tomisha tried desperately to awaken her father.

CHAPTER 21

He realized that he was having an epiphany of sorts. He had traveled this road back from Plymouth many times before, was familiar with all of its turns and indents and markings, and yet felt that he was experiencing it in a new way. The same pines and birches, the same grasslands and wild cranberry bogs, all seemed to be speaking to him now, emerging from their static shadows, alive in spirit. It was the Indian way to recognize the spirit, to separate the physical from the greater spirit. A brave kills an enemy yet honors the fighting spirit of his opponent; the hunter kills the deer yet thanks its spirit for providing meat and clothing; the squaw picks the plant and honors its gift of food. It all led logically to belief in a Great Spirit. Sassamon had concluded that the English were wrong in their approach, their external God, a God of the next world. To Sassamon it seemed that the spirits were self-evident, they were all around, one only had to open one's senses to their reality.

John Sassamon had reached the long and slow determination that, despite being Christian-trained and a Christian preacher, his belief system was still that of a Wompanoag.

It was past eight o'clock and he still had an hour or so to

go. The winter winds of January were gentle but biting and stiffly cold. He bent forward trying to lower himself against the horse's neck, pushed his hat on more tightly and shrugged his shoulders to keep his coat high against his collar line as his horse trudged through the familiar paths. All around him he could feel the dark shadows of the trees swaying forward with the wind, in cadence, emitting a sweet breezy monotone rush of sound. He found himself wondering – does the wind use the trees as its own special instrument? Or is it the spirit of the trees releasing their hidden voice through the instrument of the wind? Or both? Kindred spirits working in harmony, voices readily apparent but understood only by the introspective element of a man. Tonight was that night for John Sassamon, a night for introspection and inner spirits.

It had already been a month since Attaquin had been killed, two months since the Laphams had died. The communities had reacted in various ways, the only consistency being the anxiety that the unknown had instilled in both. Rumors were rampart, easy to start and difficult to refute. He had heard them all. Plymouth was raising a large militia force. The Laphams were developing a secret gun, powerful beyond any known armament. Philip had a thousand braves in waiting planning a coordinated surprise attack.

Both communities saw demons, both followed the natural tendency to withdraw from each other. A few optimistic representatives of both communities hoped that the various sheddings of blood could be viewed as offsetting, as recreating an equilibrium. Sassamon had hoped that would be true but, increasingly, he was convinced otherwise. He had heard the talk at the Tamarack, talk that tended to quiet in his presence. Sassamon foresaw danger, knew that isolation would breed the disease of paranoia, pressures building towards an inevitable release of some sort. A violent release he was sure. He wondered why the communities could not reach a kindred spirit as he was experiencing on his ride. Why could they not be more like the wind and the trees, coordinating together, playing off one another to form a harmonic residue.

It had been two weeks since he had been to see Metacom. He had found him to be disturbingly reflective, like a man about to unleash a change, knowing the consequences to be significant but unsure of the spread of their impact. They talked of his father – Osamequin – or "Massasoit" as the English referred to him. He related how his father came to grow fond of the name even though the term "Massasoit" referred to his position as the head of all the region's sachems and their tribes. His father had thought the English very charming and logical in mistaking his positional title for his proper name. Metacom wondered aloud just who this new Governor Winslow was – the son, Josiah Winslow, being so different from his father, former Governor Edward Winslow, who had been a good friend to Massasoit. The fathers had related well to each other; the sons seemed doomed not to.

His father was a man of his times, Metacom related, a man who saw the English as a valuable ally in the defense of his people against the constant threats of the Narragansetts, the Pequots and the powerful Mohegans. The English needed friends, his father had said, and so did his people. It had all changed now, Metacom related. Now it was the Indians who needed friends, the English who were the constant source of irritation and aggression. Our friends are among us, Metacom said, all around us. We must recognize our commonality and unite. Ominous words, Sassamon had thought, words that reflected resolution not inquiry. He had tried to nod his agreement along with Tuspaquin and the others while simultaneously trying to determine an appropriate course of action. He sensed that Metacom was not posturing, that he had decided that a defining moment had been reached.

He had labored for two days, confiding in no one, then decided that he must go to Plymouth and speak with Governor Winslow. Josiah Winslow was the son of former Governor Edward Winslow but the similarities between father and son ended at their sharing of the same office. Edward Winslow had always been a close friend of Massasoit and had been moderate in his attitudes towards the Indians. His son was a hard-liner in his attitude towards, and in his dealings with, the Wompanoags. Sassamon had always found Josiah Winslow to be a rather stiff man, formal, not given to open dialogue. Winslow had listened politely to Sassamon's concerns but had been rather dismissive. Yes, he had heard about the troubles in Middleborough and the Lakes region and, yes, it was unfortunate that so much blood had been shed. But hadn't it all been a misunderstanding, a family feud if you will, about trespassing and stolen guns? Yes, it was troubling that a radical like Tokanauset was closer to power but, in turn, Tuspaquin was also now closer to power and Tuspaquin was a sachem that could be dealt with rationally. To Winslow, Tuspaquin was a man of commerce, a man who had sold much Indian land to the English. A businessman.

Sassamon nodded respectfully and paused as Winslow poured them both another mug of hard cider. Sassamon took a long drink and then stated the words that he knew needed to be said. He believed Philip had plans of aggression and that Tuspaquin was one of Philip's prime supporters. He feared that this time the threat was not an idle one and that the potential for widespread violence was great. Winslow listened attentively but remained unconcerned, repeating his own explanation and assessment.

Sassamon had been taken aback by Winslow's response, almost as if Winslow had secret information. As his mind slid into resignation, Sassamon had donned his most formal of English manners and thanked Winslow for his time. It was obvious to both men that Sassamon had taken a precarious position in confiding his concerns, a position that put him at physical risk. A pregnant issue, one that Winslow did not acknowledge and Sassamon did not pursue. A handshake, a bow, a good wish for the new year, and Sassamon was on his way back to Middleborough.

As he neared the Nemasket village he decided that he must continue on to Assawompsett. Something at his deepest level told him that he should continue on to see his daughter, Betty, (named after her mother), and son-in-law, Felix. In payment for his many services, Tuspaquin had given him a gift of some land at the Lake – the "Neck" as it was called – and Sassamon wanted to make sure that it was properly in order so that it would pass to his daughter in the event of unfortunate circumstances. The winter wind and the long trip back from Plymouth had chilled more than his body. It had chilled his spirit and his very marrow.

CHAPTER 22

He knew it was dangerous but he could not bear to leave them. He had waited until about eleven o'clock then approached the Tamarack from the back side, had walked the final half mile through the woods so as to be unseen and had sprinted the final thirty yards from the woods, across the open corral area to the back of the barn. From there he side-stepped his way through the darkness to the rear service entrance literally sliding along the side of the barn with his back against the wall. He made his way up the rear stairs apparently unnoticed and found the door to his room. He had never recalled the door hinges being so squeaky.

Despite the obvious danger he knew that he could not leave without his books and his journal. His life had reached the point where his enemies were multiplying and his traditional sources of support were fading. It was not supposed to be like this. Men like John Sassamon were supposed to lead the new society, move seamlessly through its English and native segments, their influence determined by their ability to conduct commerce and politics in any language. Now Sassamon was dealing with unintended consequences, realizing that he had a place in neither society; that he was a figure that both societies wanted to ostracize. And minimize. And possibly eliminate. He was perceived as being devious by both the English and his own Wompanoag people, as untrustworthy, greedy. True, he had to admit, he was a bit self-absorbed and, yes, he was not bashful about personal compensation. But these were merely personal traits, minor character flaws, which should have been of lesser concern given the services that he was able to provide.

He realized his position was precarious and that he must leave … and soon. He had not made up his mind yet, possibly Mount Hope in Rhode Island to be of closer service to Metacom. Then again, increasingly he was having concerns about Metacom, gnawing doubts in his innards, a gut feel that a wise man could not ignore. No, probably Boston, maybe to Dorchester. His mind allowed him a quick repose – maybe back to Harvard. He caught himself smiling at the thought.

He found the candle dish and carefully lit the wick, placing the dish on the floor so as to minimize the light. His desk looked different to him in the reduced light, grayish and shadowy as he sat and began putting his books and papers in his worn leather satchel. Times like this made him realize just how much he loved the written word, to read and to write; to express and create. He had a gift and he felt himself most at home amongst books and papers and quills. He found his personal journal, bound in fine brown leather, his inner thoughts and musings and observations. He thought he might publish it one day, give lectures, be much in demand, an elder spokesman recalling the formative years of the new society.

His thoughts were interrupted by the muffled sounds of movement in the back hallway. Instantly, he reached down to extinguish the candle, adrenaline pouring through him, his stomach and guts churning. He could see shadows in the light just under the door, low voices, heard the turn of the latch ....

PART TWO

JUNE 8, 1675

PLYMOUTH, MASSACHUSETTS

CHAPTER 23

The three men walked silently across the courtyard, eyes blank and heads tilted forward, toward the sparse wooden gallows that had been specially constructed for their execution. Waiting for them on the gallows landing were the famed preacher, John Cotton, as well as Governor Winslow and a half dozen other officials of Plymouth Colony. Cotton waited for the three men to take their place at the side of the main stanchion. It was ten o'clock in the morning and the air was already permeated with an unseasonable humidity.

Cotton broke the crackling tension with solemn words about God's presence and His oversight of the proceedings then looked to the three accused men for a response. Tobias, the eldest and a trusted counselor to Philip, stared straight ahead, expressionless. The two younger men – Mattashunnamo and Tobias' son, Wampapaquan, fidgeted nervously, sweat pouring uncontrollably down their faces. Cotton eyed the men sternly, whispered a hushed final prayer, and motioned the executioner to begin the proceedings. Tobias was to be first. Without prodding, he stepped forward to the gallows' last planking, defiantly swiveled his head and lifted his chin. The coarse brown noose was slipped over his head and secured in a thick collar at his neck. Tobias calmly leaned forward. Cotton nodded to the executioner who then pushed Tobias out from the edge of the planking. The work was quick and clean, the neck snapping sharply, Tobias uttering a strange last sound. His body swung gently out and back, bumping against the edge of the planking, beginning to twist sideways. The executioner reached out to catch the body and gently brought it to a stop. There it hung.

After a pregnant moment, Cotton motioned for the next victim to be moved forward to the middle spot on the gallows. Mattashunnamo stiffened his shoulders, a last bit of futile resistance, and was pushed forward. A second rope was draped around his neck and he was walked to the edge. Another momentary pause, a nod from Cotton, and Mattashunnamo was pushed forward. His death was not so clean. As his body absorbed the initial shock, Mattashunnamo grunted and his shoulders jerked slightly upward, his feet reflexively kicking against air, pushing towards an invisible safe spot. Within seconds he exhaled a final sigh and his head slumped forward.

The three men had been convicted in an English court by a jury of twelve Englishmen and six Praying Indians. The sole witness had been a fellow Wompanoag named Patuckson who, from a hill overlooking Lake Assawompsett, claimed to have seen the men attack Sassamon and throw his body through a hole in the ice. There were no other witnesses, no cross examination, no other evidence … and no legal representation for the three Indians.

For Tokanauset, it all became unbearable. Standing on some higher ground in the back of the crowd with six other braves he had still retained a surreal notion that somehow the executions would be called off, that saner heads would prevail and that the English authorities would hand over the three guilty men to the Wompanoags for the implementation of native justice. The two hanging bodies fractured any semblance of that possibility. He began to move off his spot, his back to the proceedings, feeling the need for physical separation, when he heard several of his braves cry out.

"He's innocent! He's innocent! This proves it!"

Incredibly, when Wampapaquan's time had come he swung out momentarily ... and his roped snapped! Falling the five feet to the ground, he landed on one foot then went hard down onto his knees. Bolting upright, his face incredulous and filled with fright, Wampapaquan began screaming in his native tongue, incomprehensible to most of the crowd but with a message understood by all.

He was innocent ... and this miraculous event was all the proof that any God-fearing Englishmen should need!

In fact, Wampapaquan began acting like a crazed man who had just seen an apparition. He spewed out a frenzy of words, mostly in Wampanoag, some in disjointed English, insisting on his innocence. Wampapaquan then went further, implicating the two dead men as the true killers and assuring the Plymouth authorities that he had been an uninvolved bystander. Governor Winslow's face was frozen in confusion as he sought out some sort of explanation from John Cotton, who could only stare in wonder at the animated Indian. The bizarre scene ended as Wampapaquan was led away, past the two hanging bodies, incessantly proclaiming his innocence.

The other braves surrounded Tokanauset who was trying to absorb the incredible turn of events.

"He'll be let go! ... He'll be freed! ... English law says so!"

Tokanauset looked at the excited braves and broke into a broad smile.

"I believe it does."

CHAPTER 24

They left immediately for Mount Hope, Metacom's main camp and headquarters in Rhode Island, and arrived late in the afternoon of the next day. There was a strange buzz of activity, Tokanauset thought, a heightened energy. As the group entered the outer fringes of the camp, Tokanauset felt as though among strangers. In fact, the camp was filled with braves recruited by Metacom from other tribes.

Tokanauset was taken straight to Metacom's quarters, an impressive, oversized wetu that could easily hold a dozen adults. Tokanauset arrived to find the structure very crowded, overflowing with as many as twenty braves and elders. A fire burned brightly in the middle of the structure and, combined with the oppressive humidity of the day, made the wetu almost oven-like. Tokanauset felt his skin moistening as he was met by Tuspaquin and taken directly to Metacom's side.

Since his brother's death, Tokanauset had been increasingly included in tribal affairs and had been in Metacom's presence a number of times. Metacom had inherited his father, Massasoit's, size and he towered over the other attendees. Metacom was decked out in imperial clothing and adorn-

117

ments – polished buff briefs, two bright red feathers in a band around his head, plus a shiny gold trinket slung over his shoulder that he had acquired in trades with the English. Around his waist were two lengthy wampum belts. To-kanauset could not help but marvel at the exquisite colors and designs contained in the purplish shells, varied hues and carvings. Yes, his sachem was an impressive man with a powerful presence.

In his limited dealings with Metacom, Tokanauset had found him to be a bit distant. Wary. Cautious. Perhaps, To-kanauset had thought, it was due to Metacom's unfamiliarity with him. But today proved to be different. Metacom welcomed him warmly, extended his large hand to To-kanauset and grasped his forearm against his own in a gesture of brotherhood. He was anxious to hear of the events in Plymouth and Tokanauset related the details of yesterday's incredible happening. Metacom listened intently, saying nothing and giving no hint of reaction. Finally, he rose and stood towering over the group.

"My brothers," he started. "Yesterday, the English threw a large stone into a pond. Our pond. The pond that we all share as brothers. They have taken justice into their own hands, justice that rightly belonged to us. Justice in the case of an internal Indian affair - an Indian victim and Indian perpetrators and an Indian accuser. They have determined that the Wompanoag system of justice stands second to their own legal system. Yesterday, the English enforced their legal system on us, killing two of us including Tobias."

Most in the group had known Tobias as a loyal and trusted confidant of Metacom's. While they were aware that Tobias had been found guilty, they were also aware that, prior to the trial, Metacom had gone to Plymouth as a gesture of good faith and to explain that he, himself, had had no involvement in the death of John Sassamon. Most had assumed that the English would somehow reciprocate the trust Metacom had shown their authorities. Metacom's announcement brought audible gasps from a number of the group.

"We are many now. And stronger every day. We grow in numbers, bonded by our brotherhood." He stopped to let his words be absorbed. "What has been taken from us can no longer continue. Soon, our braves will begin the war dance and we will seek the guidance of those that have gone before us."

Metacom let his eyes work the message, moving to each of them.

"There will be many ripples from this English stone!" he thundered.

The group erupted in emotion, heads nodding vigorously, hand clasps and body hugs being exchanged. The group began to move outside and the traditional beating of drums started up. As Tokanauset moved to follow the group out the wetu's opening he felt a large hand grasp him on the forearm. Only he and Tuspaquin and Metacom remained in the wetu. Metacom motioned for them to stay.

The three sat near the fire, sweating profusely. Metacom reached behind him and brought forth a large pipe that was still smoldering. He turned the pipe to the fire and revived the burning tobacco then handed the pipe to Tuspaquin.

The wetu grew silent as each man puffed.

"Now is our time," he stated absently.

Tuspaquin absorbed the comment for a moment.

"Your father would understand … and he would agree."

Metacom tilted his body away from the fire and let his head fall back onto his neck, as if looking skyward. He exhaled deeply.

"Yes, you are right. … We are right. He would agree. … It is time for "King Philip" to act!"

Metacom and Tuspaquin could see that Tokanauset was puzzled and they exchanged smirky little grins with each other.

"Yes Tokanauset, you are in the presence of a king."

Metacom then related to Tokanauset the origin of the reference. A dozen or so years before, in 1662, the English had summoned Metacom to Plymouth to answer concerns about Indian unrest and rumors about war preparations. Upon their father Massasoit's death in 1660, Metacom's older brother Wamsutta had assumed the position of sachem. Almost immediately, Wamsutta found himself at odds with the Plymouth authorities concerning disputes about land sales. Shortly thereafter, Wamsutta died under mysterious circumstances while at the home of some Plymouth authorities in Marshfield. It was widely contended in Indian circles that Wamsutta had been poisoned. Interestingly, before his death, Wamsutta had acted upon a recommendation from his scribe and interpreter that he and his brother Metacom should change their names to "Alexander" and "Philip" respectively.

The interpreter's name was John Sassamon.

Metacom went on to describe his appearance at the Plymouth court. When he appeared before the Plymouth authorities he insisted that the English had no jurisdiction over him or his people. In fact, Metacom was adamant that he should be considered in the same stature as the English king, Charles II, to whom the Plymouth representatives were subject. Metacom was aware that, from that day, many of the English referred to him in mocking reference as the "king".

He had found the reference to be amusing and came to like it.

Metacom smiled whimsically at the completion of the story. He looked over at Tuspaquin.

"Your son-in-law; my lost 'son'", and the two men began howling in laughter. Recognizing Tokanauset's confusion, this time it was Tuspaquin who explained the reference.

"As our 'king' and his wife had their first son, they had a desire to make sure that certain things were made clear particularly the baby's inheritance of certain lands."

Metacom interrupted him. "A 'will', I believe the English call it."

"Yes, a will." Tuspaquin went on. "It seems the will read

121

one way when Sassamon read it back but somehow got changed as it was to become official."

Metacom tilted his head back smiling. "No doubt Sassamon would have been a good sachem with all that land he willed himself." He blew out a long breath. "Very unchristian of him."

The drums were now beating incessantly, the traditional whoops and cries of the ceremony becoming a crescendo. With a nod towards the doorway, Metacom motioned that they should join the multitudes outside. He stood up, paused a moment, and looked warmly upon both men.

To Tuspaquin he said simply, "Bring me the tongue of that fellow Patuckson."

He turned his full attention now to Tokanauset.

"Our actions begin tomorrow," Metacom said in a whisper. "You have a warrior's heart. I – and your people – have need of your services."

Tokanauset felt the request sear into him, a private and personal announcement from the head sachem that their world was about to come undone. Steeled, Tokanauset looked Metacom directly in the eye and vigorously nodded his acceptance.

CHAPTER 25

The war party trudged purposefully towards Swansea, only about five miles from their Mount Hope encampment. They were ten strong, prepared for war yet unsure how to enact it. The road before them was familiar to a number of them, a daily part of their travel rituals. In fact, the English neighbors of Mount Hope had been always accommodating to Indian needs and concerns. They had done an effective job of keeping their animals fenced and contained. On those occasions when their cows and pigs broke loose and trampled the Indian corn plantings, the English in this area inevitably tried to make a fair restitution. Yet Metacom had decreed that actions against the English were to begin.

From a distance they could see two English houses, one far to their right nearest the coast and one to their left, further inland. Looking left, they could make out two figures at the inland house, one on horseback and another who appeared to be loading tools into a wagon. They could see no activity at the coastal house and, in fact, not even any smoke from its chimney. They decided to split into two groups and approach the coastal house from its front and its back. Fifteen minutes later, both groups lay in separate woods contemplating their next action.

Finally, one of the braves from the rear group leaped forward and raced towards the house. He ran evasively through open ground, fearing gunfire, until he reached the corral fence. Contained inside were a number of cows and sheep. The brave continued into the barn followed now by three others. They found the barn empty. The two that had flintlocks readied them for firing and the other two brandished their sharpened tomahawks. Stealthily, they approached the main door. Taking cover, one of them called out in a subdued war cry, a half warning, half invitation. From the other side they could see the second group of their party approaching the house now, fully exposed, and drawing no fire. They realized that the house was abandoned and they began entering. One of the braves found a straw broom and moved towards the hearth where the barest smoldering of embers could be found. He breathed evenly on the embers, stoking them with kindling, until he had a small fire re-ignited. Others found articles of clothing which they tied together. The first brave stuck the broom over the fire and watched as it ignited. He looked gleefully at his companions then raced out of the house's front door. The others set the articles of clothing on fire and placed the flaming objects around the inside of the house. As they all ran outside they could see that the first brave had successfully ignited the barn on fire. The group moved off a safe distance, perhaps thirty yards or so, and watched the results of their handiwork. The barn, fueled by stores of dry hay and seed, erupted in a crackling, searing ball of angry yellow-orange. The house soon followed.

Giddy with their success the group let out a variety of war cries. The brave who had led the first group yelled out for them to attack the inland house and they all ran excitedly through the woods to connect back out to the main road.

Their progress was halted when they heard the sound of two gunshots. Looking back, they could see that two of the cows had been shot and lay toppled on the ground. They watched in amusement as the other three braves raised their tomahawks and chased the sheep around the pen.

From atop Mount Hope, Metacom stood alone and surveyed the wide landscape that extended before him. As the flames and smoke became prominent on his right he turned and smiled at Tuspaquin, Tokanauset and the other assembled leaders. Soon a corresponding inferno was visible on the left.

King Philip's War had begun.

CHAPTER 26

As had become their want, Thomas and Edward had led the company on another of its operations. They had been with the company for five months and, when in the field, had come to realize that there was no shortage of fools in either the lead positions or the leadership positions. When it came to seeking out a hidden enemy – or avoiding one – they had an inherent trust in their own finely honed instincts for hunting. Other of their peers came to have the same appreciation and the two willingly accepted the responsibility.

It was already late November with its dark, early sunsets and cool, stiff nights. The company was patrolling in the swamps outside of Rehobeth having been told that a number of Indians were in the area likely protecting a winter hideout. They were under the overall command of James Cudworth but, increasingly, they served under the direction of one Colonel Samuel Moseley. Moseley was actually a sea captain - some said a pirate – and he was assisted by a huge Dutchman named Cornelius Anderson.

Together, they had recruited a number of ruffians from Boston and an eclectic battle group was formed, a combination of wild, urban men of questionable reputation and simple farm boys of considerable hunting skill. It made for a surprisingly effective fighting force.

On this day it was mid afternoon and the sky was showing its first sign of darkening. Thomas and Edward had suggested that they go ahead of the company, circling around to the right of the suspected hideout and away from the natural approach that the Indians might assume any English contingent would take. As was their habit, each carried two flintlocks, rifles of their own creation crafted at the Lapham mill complex. Thomas led them, Edward trailing ten yards behind him, both crawling on their bellies through thick growth. While difficult and painstaking, it afforded virtual secrecy to the two men. Also with them was a young soldier they knew only as William who was to be the runner who would relay information back to Colonel Moseley.

Edward saw Thomas stop and motion him to move forward. Through the thick brush they could see the winter village about a hundred yards ahead of them. The trees thinned out between their position and that of the village leaving a relatively open field of wild grass ahead of them. The village was elevated a bit on a slight plateau giving its inhabitants an excellent vantage point. Their position was to the right of the village while the main body of Moseley's men was to their left. The field of wild grasses extended sideways, in front of Moseley's forces as well, meaning that any attack would require the force to cross open ground.

Thomas saw that perhaps fifty yards ahead of them was a rock that rose about two feet above the ground and had some thin shrubbery growing beside it. He suggested that Edward cover him and he would attempt to crawl to the rock. Edward grabbed his arm.

"Don't! We don't know how many of them there are. You could get stuck out there."

Edward glanced over at William who looked entranced at the opportunity to see real, battle-hardened soldiers at work. Edward handed him one of his rifles.

"You know how to load one of these?"

William eyed the flintlock, turned it sideways and nodded affirmatively.

"OK, first, we wait here until we can figure out how many of them there are. They are already in our range. We have four shots among us and the kid can get us two more ..."

Edward stopped in mid-sentence as two Indians approached the outer confines of the village near the edge of the grassy field. One of the Indians plopped down into a sitting position against a tree trunk, looking back towards the village. The other Indian remained standing and began to relieve himself, apparently to the consternation of the sitting Indian who bolted sideways. Both shared a laugh at the prank then went silent as a third Indian approached them, appearing to share a message. None of the three Indians seemed to be carrying any weapons.

From behind them, Edward and Thomas heard sharp rustlings. In an instant, Edward had seized the rifle from William's hands, rolled to his left and turned onto his stomach in a firing position. Thomas had done likewise taking a kneeling position behind a small shrub. From less than five feet in front of them emerged a member of Moseley's staff to face a dumbfounded William and two fully engaged rifles pointed directly at him.

"Moseley wants to go in. He's out of patience," the messenger said nervously, eyeing the flintlock that Thomas had kept trained on him.

Edward and Thomas exchanged glances of disgust and Thomas finally lowered his weapon. Both knew that the decision had already been made.

"Tell Moseley that, so far, we have only seen three of them. The village appears quiet. We'll give you five minutes to get back. We will take out the two sentries and then move across. Wait for our shots! Tell Moseley to head straight across in a concentrated line. Don't spread out! The Indians only have a limited firing point from where they are so can likely be overpowered by a mass of men."

Edward handed the weapon back to William as Thomas gave one final admonition.

"For God's sake, go quietly."

CHAPTER 27

F ive minutes had passed and it was time for action. To Thomas, the field had taken on an eerie silence, as if they were being watched. As if the Indians had found a way to float above them, invisible, waiting to strike. He had seen their capabilities, knew their cunning, their warrior spirit. "One Englishman is worth twenty Indians; only ten if he's drunk," went the old saw. Thomas and Edward had both seen how foolhardy such "wisdom" could be.

The plan was that both of them would fire then the three of them would sprint to the rock to re-load and assess the situation. From there they could provide angular fire in support of Moseley's frontal assault. Each made a final check of their weapon, decided on their target and assumed a shooting position.

They fired simultaneously, a cracking double boom that echoed across the open field and reverberated through the woods. Edward's shot had thumped into the chest of the standing Indian, felling him in his place. Thomas aimed at the sitting Indian and watched as his cheek exploded in a burst of bright crimson spray. The sitting Indian was knocked forward, face first onto his stomach and reflexively began crawling ahead. To their left they could see the first of Moseley's men swarming across the open field, a wild, shouting mass of fury.

As the three men arrived at the rock, Edward began the reloading process and Thomas scanned back into the village anticipating Indian reinforcements to rush forward. To his surprise, only women and children began to emerge from the wetus, curious as to the noise. The third Indian that they had seen was nowhere in sight.

The first of Moseley's men were now across and sprinting through the last of the trees that shielded the village. Thomas cringed as he saw one of the men slash his sword down and into the back of the Indian that he had shot. In the village, women and children continued to emerge from the wetus. Many instinctively pushed their children back inside the structures. Others began running for their life towards the rear of the village and into the surrounding swamp. The first shots started to ring out as Moseley's troops began gunning down any of the Indians that remained outside. Into this maelstrom rode Moseley and his second, Cornelius Anderson.

"Well done boys, we've had them today! Dig them out of the swamps, every last one of them!"

Edward and Thomas walked the last fifty yards across the field and entered the village.

"Nice of you to join us!" boomed Moseley. "What took you so Goddamn long?"

In their peripheral vision Edward and Thomas could see the

first of the wetus being set ablaze.

"What are they doing?" screamed Edward, beseeching Moseley and Anderson to stop the arson. "There is food in this village, all kinds of food! Tell them to stop!"

Anderson dismounted from his horse and stepped towards Edward, stopping only inches away from him. Physically, Anderson towered over most of the men and intimidation was a prime method in his command style.

Anderson bent slightly at the knees so that his face was directly in front of Edward's.

"Going a little soft on us, are you Mister Innkeeper?" he sneered.

Edward would have none of his guff, was hardened to combat and to combat circumstances.

"This is a supply village! There is food all around us. Shelter too."

Moseley now interjected himself into the confrontation. He was seething at Edward's comments, dangerously angry, the tense situation deteriorating.

"Indian food! Indian shelter! What are you thinking you bloody fool! I should tan your arse for such a dumb idea! We are Englishmen, you shit!"

With that Moseley wheeled his horse, Anderson following.

"Fire them all boys!"

The unruly mob of men did not have to be told twice. Soon the air was filled with the crackle of blazing pines and pods of smoke from each ignition. Unable to stand the heat that now emanated from the center of the village, the men roamed the outer perimeter laughing and boisterous.

Edward and Thomas entered one of the last wetus and immediately found the location of its provisions. While they were inside, a group of three soldiers entered and were about to set fire to the wetu. Thinking quickly, Thomas said, "Hold on. Moseley told us to save one for himself." Satisfied, the men left. Edward and Thomas then filled their pockets with as much of the dried corn and smoked deer meat as they could hold.

The two men emerged from the wetu and moved fifty yards off to the side to escape the heat. They chewed on the corn in silence. Finally, Edward took a last gulp and spit out an accumulation of husk remnants.

"My friend, I'm not sure I can last much longer under this Moseley bastard. I am seriously thinking that a third eye would become him." He shouldered his flintlock and simulated its firing. A satisfied smile spread across his face.

"I'm also counting on you to take out the big jackass."

Thomas could only laugh. It was dark now and both watched as the undisciplined troops moved shadow-like among the smoldering village.

"We're lucky to be serving with such heroes."

CHAPTER 28

The June day had broken warm and sunny, a pleasant diversion from the rains that had consistently soaked the troops over the past week. Almost a year of fighting had hardened the troops to certain realities, a prominent one being that one took the sun and the heat wherever and whenever one could find it. The men were listless and only desired to draw a little warmth and dryness into their soggy woolen trousers and their stinking shoes. There were a total of about twenty of them, out in the open along the banks of the Taunton River looking for some Godforsaken way across the water in pursuit of some Godforsaken Indians in some Godforsaken part of the outskirts of Plymouth Colony.

Charles Lapham, a captain now, rode his horse straight into a group of a dozen men trying to get them energized and focused. His efforts were interrupted by the dismissive words of the commander, Amos Churchill.

"Leave them be, Lapham!" Churchill intoned. "Well boys, a good day to dry out the old manhood!" With that, Churchill laughed heartily and rode back into the coolness of the woods. Charles Lapham followed him closely.

"Sir, with all due respect, I think we need a bit more order and readiness."

"Relax Lapham! The war's over! We've had 'em on the run all winter, all spring too. They're out of food, out of munitions … out of will. Besides, there's twenty of us. Twenty Englishmen. Some with "Lapham" guns, for God's sake. That's worth a hundred Indians … and we'd have to go all the way to Mount Hope to find that many Indian fighters."

Churchill pulled out a small metal flask and took a deep drink from its liquid. He offered it to Charles, who politely refused, then took another quick hit for himself.

"By the way, Mount Hope might be around the next bend for all I know. Where the hell are we?"

Charles diplomatically explained their location to Churchill who seemed only half interested. Charles owed his military commission to Churchill, a commission that was very important to him. Being an officer would no doubt enhance his prospects for the lucrative political career on which his sights were set.

"Sir, it looks like we have found the shallowest point in the river so we should cross here. The scouts say there is a village a few miles inland that might be a supply depot of some sort."

"Fine. Fine. Let's have at it then."

CHAPTER 29

The men were not at all excited about the exhortations they were receiving from Captain Lapham and they groused noisily at the prospects of continuing their march. The rocky bed of the river was exposed a bit more than normal for springtime and provided warming supports on which to stretch out and rest. Such small comforts were not easily taken from hardened soldiers.

Charles ordered the men broken up into three groups – five, five and ten. The river was low, exposing about twenty yards of mud on either side before the thick woods reasserted control of the landscape. The plan was for the first group of five men to cross to the other side, infiltrate the woods, and establish a lookout of protection while the second and third groups crossed.

From his horse, Charles directed the first group across.

"First group, begin. And for God's sake try and keep the noise down."

More grousing, low, profane responses, one soldier laughing and deliberately churning the water, knees high, in great splashes, to the delight of the others. Without waiting for Charles' order, the second group began crossing haphazardly. Charles had no choice but to follow and insert himself among them.

One of the soldiers was next to the splashing man, enjoying the reverie and he proceeded to fall face first into the water, pitching forward towards the far bank. Charles felt his gut sicken as he recognized a familiar sound through the noise of the choppy waters. The splashing man then turned towards Charles, a horrified look on his face and a swatch of bright red bursting from his neck. Charles heard two more pings and then the thump of an arrow hitting one of his troopers in the chest and knocking him backwards into Charles' horse.

They were being ambushed.

CHAPTER 30

From his position across the river about fifty yards into the woods, Tokanauset could see his plan unfolding perfectly. He had been made aware that the English force was in the area and he had anticipated that they would eventually look for a low point at which to ford the river. He had hoped that the English would find this one.

He had placed two volunteers on the other side armed with flintlocks. Their orders were to wait for the appointed signal – a bird warble – then fire into the rear of the English contingent and sprint downstream away from the action. If their timing was right Tokanauset hoped that he could get the English to hurry forward away from the perceived attack coming from their rear and into his waiting group of ten braves. His men had only two guns among them and Tokanauset had chosen to place them both on the far side of the river to accomplish the desired effect.

It had worked to perfection.

As the English crossed sloppily he could see that none of his men had been detected. Two of his men were heavily camouflaged and were within five yards of the first woody vegetation. The splashing from the soldier caused him his one moment of concern, that his signal would be unheard. Tokanauset made an instantaneous decision to send one of his men through the woods down about twenty yards to his right and have that man give the warble.

Two of his men had bows and each placed an arrow that knocked down one of the Englishmen. His remaining braves sprang forward out of the woods and into the open, piercing the air with battle yells and hurling hatchets and knives into the thickening confusion of Englishmen. Two braves remained next to Tokanauset awaiting his instructions. Despite the din of the battle, Tokanauset instinctively directed them with silent gestures and whispered commands. Amused, one of his braves pointed out that it was now safe to talk in normal tones.

As they stood strategizing, they could see one of the English soldiers streaking towards them, wide-eyed and petrified with fear, shouting incoherent phrases and racing toward some unseen safe haven. Somehow the soldier – a boy really - had made it through the Indian contingent and was racing uncontrollably toward an imagined freedom. The two braves looked knowingly at each other. As the soldier approached them, one of the braves threw his body into the upper thighs of the boy sending him sprawling to the ground. Instantly, the other brave was on the stunned Englishman holding him by the collar of his shirt with one hand and the mane of his hair with the other. The first Indian had sprung to his feet and placed his face directly in front of the terrified soldier, mumbling words that were incomprehensible to him. From behind, the second Indian raised his knife and deftly sliced into the soldier's forehead at the hairline, plunging deep into the scalp and tearing back a swatch of skin and hair with a burst of bright red blood. The soldier emitted a bloodcurdling scream, a second, then collapsed to the ground in an excruciating spasm of pain.

Needing to regain focus, in the midst of the soldier's death throes, Tokanauset mercifully crushed his skull with his tomahawk.

Tokanauset turned his attention back to the frothing action taking place in the middle of the river and it was then that he noticed the mounted figure, swirling, trying to get control of his horse and his men. The size of the man made him unmistakable. Tokanauset felt a delicious smile overtaking his face and he gave a quick prayer of thanks to the spirits for this incredible good fortune. Losing all pretense of self-control, Tokanauset felt his face flush with the excitement of battle. He bellowed out a fierce war cry and propelled himself forward towards the saddled figure.

CHAPTER 31

C harles desperately tried to rally his soldiers who were all around him falling in confusion, struck by arrows and knives and unsure in which direction to run. Charles had all he could do to control the wild bucking of his horse and he could not focus on the direction of the attack. The scene around him was one of panic and chaos as his men churned up the river in a frenzied attempt to flee, amidst curses and screams of fear. From the stream of crazed men that were rushing past him Charles could sense that they must retreat to the shore from which they had come.

As he wheeled his horse back to the original river bank he felt the hot slicing of the knife into his upper thigh. Instinctively he kicked at the brave who was trying to lift his leg out of the stirrup to throw him off the horse. The brave had been able to get his boot out when Charles felt the thud of the tomahawk on the back of his head. His body involuntarily lurched forward, out of the saddle, as he tried to hold on to the horse's mane. He felt himself losing control then finally plunging downwards into the cold stream. He scrambled up from the water, got to one knee and attempted to lurch forward when he felt the crush of the blow. It knocked him ahead, out of the water and onto the rocky landing. He felt movement around him as he began to lose consciousness. He collapsed to the ground, on his knees, his mind moving to an inner place, an inner chamber, where the only clear sounds were of his own breathing, all other sounds being muffled and incomprehensible. Then he felt himself on his back, looking up into bright sky, his bearings turning on him in a slow swirl, his vision wet and filmy from his fall.

As he looked up a final time he saw a familiar face framed against the crystal blue sky. His mind struggled for meaning as he saw the face look upward, thrusting something in the air amidst a scream that Charles could see but not hear. Then he saw the knife and the ferocious face, recognized, saw the knife begin its descent, time slowing, saw the glint, a quick vision of Rachel, accepted the inevitability, closed his eyes tightly, braced for the impact.

CHAPTER 32

I t had taken three days but they had almost made it back to Middleborough. They had started as a group of eight and had taken great care in their travel. But after the first day, the shock of the new reality had become clear. They had encountered no Indians and realized that their concerns had been unnecessary. There were no Indians to be found. There were no English to be found. There were no animals to be found. Only devastation. Destruction. Charcoal ash where houses had once stood; Indian villages reduced to burnt rubble. Animal carcasses in various states of decay, the stink fueled by the July heat. The eerie silence was disturbing to them. And compelling. Mesmerizing. They were wanderers in a new world.

They had left Moseley's unit on July 1st, not really dismissed but not really deserting. It was just time. The fighting had slowed considerably over the past two months. Losses on both sides had been devastating but particularly for the Indians. Various Indian tribes had made a separate peace with the English, some turning sides, some just withdrawing from the combat.

Increasingly, Philip and his shrinking forces were isolated and contained to their primary base near Mount Hope.

There were plenty on the English side that were determined to see the combat through to its inevitable conclusion, the death of Philip. Others, like Thomas and Edward, were only interested in going home to whatever remained of their previous lives. They had been in service for a year, had witnessed incalculable suffering and loss, their idyllic youth fractured. They had been participants, recipients and perpetrators. They were tired. They had had enough.

Thomas had been advised the previous week that Charles had died in combat. Edward had been very concerned with how sullen Thomas had become and it was Edward who suggested that they just up and leave. The pursuit of Philip was heading towards Rhode Island and their home lay in the opposite direction. Their work was done, Edward had argued. It was time to go.

They had fought for a year with the comfort that their families were relatively safe in Plymouth. Rachel and the children had been taken there at Charles' insistence. John Horton and his family had stubbornly remained at the Tamarack feeling that they had a certain amount of goodwill within the local Indian community. But a tense confrontation with a band of Indians who he did not recognize made Horton realize that this was a regional conflict. Begrudgingly, he joined the last caravan that Charles had escorted to Plymouth before leaving for his combat assignment.

Thomas and Edward led two other companions along the familiar roads that would take them to the Tamarack. Already, they could feel cooling breezes from off the lake and they quickened their step. They had been warned of the destruction and had been given no reason for hope otherwise. Still, Edward's face brightened as he anticipated seeing his home.

Reality quickly set in for him.

CHAPTER 33

The four men swung onto the main road that ran along Lake Assawompsett, the water being to their left, and headed towards the Tamarack. Edward quick-stepped ahead of the group and the men watched him stop dead in his tracks and emit an audible gasp. Ahead of them stood the remnants of the two story structure, a seared and blackened tangle of burnt beams interspersed amidst piles of dirt and debris. The remains of the three stone chimneys stood erect and symmetrical to one another while, all around, pieces of wall supports and cross beams were linked in skeletal disarray. All were charred and disfigured, almost gothic in appearance. Behind, they could see the remains of the barn, a collapsed mass of brown and black hubris. The men spread out and each began a silent meandering through the wreckage. Near one of the chimneys Edward found the remains of pots and dishes, many still whole and in reasonable condition. It appeared that the building had been torched from outside and not ransacked. He took some comfort in that notion.

Near the barn and corral area the findings were a bit more grisly. Scattered about were the remains of various animals, apparently shot or hacked to death. There was no telling exactly when the incendiary action had taken place but it had not been recently. Already, grasses and mossy growths were appearing throughout, a tribute to nature's ability to regenerate amid chaos. Edward could only stare, absorbing the scene, his mind retreating to a private place. Thomas approached him from the rear and the two stood abreast in silence. After a few moments, Edward looked over at his friend, his mouth opening. He held this pose for a moment, struggling for words, then began shaking his head in resignation, emitting a long exhale. Thomas nodded his head slowly, deliberately, three, four, five times, in quiet empathy, finally letting out a long breath of his own and turning to leave. Edward remained stationary, took in one final observation, then turned and followed the three men back out onto the main road.

They walked in silence, headed towards the center of Middleborough, towards the Lapham mill complex. Along the way, a journey of about five miles, they passed other scenes of destruction, the ugly, burnt, dilapidated remains of men at war. The half dozen dwellings that constituted the center of Middleborough were all completely destroyed, each its own brown-black maze of cinder. Leaving the center they were soon at the crest of the hill that looked down upon the Nemasket River and the Lapham complex. This time Thomas was allowed the respect of viewing first. Perception met reality, the complex was completely destroyed.

As they made their way down the hill and across the river they could see only the stone walls that had once been the support for the main structure. The top of the water wheel had been burnt in place, giving the eerie impression of a blackened hulk that appeared to be floating on the water. Thomas headed to inspect the water wheel but his steps were interrupted by the sound of men wielding their flint-

locks. There was also the distinct sound of a man wretch-
ing. Thomas hustled around the wall that had once been the
front of the saw mill, to the stone building in which he and
Edward had spent so much time working their craft. He
saw Edward on his knees, his head tilted to his side and
bent low, emptying the contents of his stomach. The other
two men stood with their guns poised. They looked dazed,
star struck.

In front of them, leaning against the stone building, were
four poles. On top of the poles, withered, brown and dark,
were the remains of a human head, a scalp, and two hands.

Thomas felt his stomach churn, felt his heart surge in reaction. He let out a long, sustained, guttural cry of agony and
disbelief as he raced to the poles.

It was Charles.

Thomas lost all semblance of control as the horrifying reality seared into his being.

"No! No! Noooooooooohhhhh!" he wailed, primal in intensity. "Noooooooooohhhhh! ...... No ....no."

He could feel himself crashing ..... overwhelmed .....
draining. He fell limply to the ground, the others trying to
support him, Edward trying to comfort him, his hands on
Thomas' shoulders. Thomas could only sit, cross legged,
arms folded across his body, hugging himself, rocking ...
rocking ... rocking.

"Enough!" he whimpered. "Enough. .... Enough."

Edward took a kneeling position directly behind his friend, his hands on his shoulders, rocking in rhythm, a face of pain, silent, sharing.

Minutes passed, time irrelevant, muting into complete silence. At last Thomas rose to his feet, his face awash in tears, eyes raw and filmed over. He approached the poles and eyed them through watery, opaque lenses. He slipped off his shirt and laid it on the ground. Then, gently, reverently, he reached up and took the head of his brother off the pole and laid it on the shirt. He gathered the other remains, kneeled in front of the garment, his eyes covered by tears, and slowly, meticulously, he pulled up at the edges until he had a bundle that he could carry.

He looked at Edward.

"Let's go," he whispered softly.

PART THREE

AUGUST 18, 1676

LAKEVILLE, MASSACHUSETTS

CHAPTER 34

A s they approached the Tamarack, they both broke into spontaneous smiles. From the second floor staging Edward had caught sight of the carriage and had been waving furiously. He bounded down to the ground, a giddy look on his face and sprinted to the carriage. Sarah had jumped down herself, not waiting for the usual courtesy from her husband who was otherwise engaged in a bear hug with his brother-in-law.

"Looks good!" Thomas laughed.

Edward made his way over to his sister for a kiss and spun her towards the reconstructed building.

"Coming along!" he shouted.

Thomas led the horses and carriage over to a hitching post as Edward walked arm-in-arm with his sister towards a carpentry area.

"Look at this!" he exclaimed, puffed with pride. There, almost completed, was a massive oaken door that would soon adorn the front of the building. The carpenter pulled away from his work revealing that he had almost completed carving the name into the door.

Edward grinned broadly, no words necessary.

"Father said you were coming by. You sure you don't want to stay around a few more days?"

Thomas and Sarah both looked at each other and smiled.

"No. We're anxious to get settled. I've got that place in mind that I told you about over in Titticut, towards Bridgewater, where the river does the loop. She's heard me talk a lot about it. It's time for her to see it."

They had been married for just over a week.

Edward and Thomas had made their way to Plymouth for the tearful reunion with their families. They had come back as men, changed, hardened. They had learned the meaning of precious and the limits of time. As they arrived in Plymouth, Sarah had seen him first and had lost all pretense. She raced to him, a release of pent up feelings. Thomas did likewise. He asked for her hand and her father happily agreed.

Their marriage took place in the newly rebuilt church at the Green, the first marriage performed in the new facility. After the ceremony, the parties had moved across the street and laid flowers at the graves of Leroy, Arby and Charles. August had been a time of good news for Plymouth Colony. Philip had been cornered near Mount Hope and killed and, while pockets of Indian resistance remained, the war was effectively over. It was a time of new beginnings.

THE SASSAMON CIRCLE

"Have you changed your mind about the mill?

Thomas did not hesitate.

"No. Word is out that interested parties should come to see you about the property. If you hear of any takers then let them know it is theirs."

The two friends squared off to each other, Thomas extending his hand.

"The mill is located on angry ground. I'm just looking for a quiet piece of land."

The two embraced. Thomas turned to the carriage, winked up at Sarah, then spun back to Edward and laughed.

"You know, I never really liked working with wood."

EPILOGUE

The real John Sassamon died on January 29, 1675 under mysterious circumstances and his body was found under the ice of Lake Assawompsett in Lakeville, MA. In March of that same year, three Wompanoag Indians, all loyal to Philip (Metacom), were brought to trial in Plymouth, and, in June, were convicted and executed for the murder.

The circumstances surrounding the trial and the execution were as I have described them in this book. The men had been tried in an English court but without the benefit of many of the established principles of English law. They were denied legal counsel and were not allowed to cross examine the prosecutor's sole witness, an Indian named Patuckson. Patuckson claimed to have seen the attack from a hill above the lake. A jury of twelve Englishmen and six Praying Indians heard the case and rendered the verdict.

One of the accused was a Wompanoag named Tobias who was a known friend and counselor to Philip. Prior to the trial, Tobias was released on bail, bail that was posted by Tuspaquin. This put Tuspaquin in the unusual position of posting bail for the release of the man who was accused of murdering his son-in-law.

There were various speculations as to what had happened
to John Sassamon. Some thought that he might have com-
mitted suicide while others thought that he may have had a
heart attack or other medical condition that caused him to
fall into an ice fishing hole. Sassamon would have been
about 55 years of age at the time. The Indians who saw his
body under the ice pulled him out and immediately buried
him near the shore of Lake Assawompsett. They had found
Sassamon's gun, hat, and a brace of ducks on the surface of
the lake.

The Wompanoag attacks on towns in southeastern Massachusetts began on June 19th. Fourteen months later, on August 12th, 1676, Philip was cornered and killed by colonial
forces. The war lasted another month, ending in September,
1676.

In his book **Igniting King Philip's War : The John Sassamon Murder Trial**, Yasuhide Kawashima writes :

> *"The trial of the suspected murderers gave a new (and
> to the Indians) ominous spin to the tug of war over In-
> dian allegiance and identity. By insisting that the death
> of a Wompanoag Indian, supposedly at the hands of
> other Wampanoags, be resolved in a colonial court, the
> Plymouth magistrates were announcing that the Wom-
> panoag people could no longer employ their own meth-
> ods of fact finding and retribution. The trial thus denied
> to the Wompanoags the last shreds of their independ-
> ence as a people and a culture.*

> *Seen in this multi-layered context, the death of Sassa-
> mon and the trial of his suspected killers were of the
> utmost importance for the colonists and the Indians. It*

highlighted basic and intractable issues of identity and authority. Given its outcome, one may wonder whether King Philip's War was not inevitable. And perhaps justifiable as well?"

The King Philip's War had devastating consequences to both the English settlers and the native population of southeastern Massachusetts. Proportionate to the population, the number of English deaths represented the highest fatality rate of any war in which the United States has participated. Many towns, including Middleborough, were set afire and completely destroyed in the attacks. Indian losses, both on the battlefield and as a result of disease, were cataclysmic.

In his book **Mayflower,** John Philbrick writes (page 332) :

"In terms of the percentage of the population killed, the English had suffered casualties that are difficult for us to comprehend today. During the forty five months of World War Two, the United States lost just under 1 percent of its adult male population; during the Civil War the casualty rate was somewhere between 4 and 5 percent; during the fourteen months of King Philip's War, Plymouth Colony lost close to 8 percent of its men.

But the English losses appear almost inconsequential when compared to those of the Indians. Of a total Native population of approximately 20,000, at least 2000 had been killed in battle or died of their injuries; 3000 had died of sickness or starvation, 1000 had been shipped out of the country as slaves, while an estimated 2000 eventually fled ... Overall, the Native American population of southern New England had sustained a

LOUIS GARAFALO

loss of somewhere between 60 and 80 percent. Philip's local squabble with Plymouth Colony had mutated into a region wide war that, on a percentage basis, had done nearly as much as the plagues of 1616 – 1619 to decimate New England's Native population."

There was a time in southeastern Massachusetts when both societies – English and Native American - though eyeing each other warily, considered the settlement of a mixed society quite possible and maybe even desirable. History could have turned out much differently.

AUTHOR'S NOTE

This is a work of fiction with fictional characters and events. Having said that, many of the characters in this book did actually exist and the setting of certain scenes in the Middleboro and Lakeville areas of Massachusetts can still be visited today.

The characters of Leroy Lapham, Iona Lapham, Charles, Thomas and Arby (Leroy Junior) Lapham as well as Agnes and Earl Lapham are all fictional. In all honesty, the names Leroy Lapham, Iona Lapham and Arby Lapham belonged to my maternal grandfather, grandmother and uncle although their characterization in the book bears no resemblance to their actual personalities or physical appearance when they were alive (all are deceased). Likewise the characters of Edward Horton, Sarah Horton and John Horton are fictional. Finally, the characters of Attaquin, Tokanauset and Tomisha are all fictional.

The Tamarack was once a longstanding restaurant / pub in Lakeville, MA and the "tamarack" area still exists around Lake Assawompsett. One can still visit the "muttock" area of Middleboro which is bisected by the Nemasket River. The site of the Lapham sawmill was inspired by the Oliver Mill Park, owned by colonial judge Peter Oliver and located on the Nemasket River in Middleborough.

Certain of the characters in the story were real people. Pamontaquash was known as the "pond sachem" and is believed to be the father of Tuspaquin, who was known as the "black sachem". There is a small lake in Middleborough named after Tuspaquin. Colonel Benjamin Church was a real militia figure in the King Philip War. Edward and Josiah Winslow were father and son and both served as the governor of Plymouth Colony, Josiah starting in 1672. Francis Coombs was a town official in Middleboro at this time and later served as one of Middleborough's first selectmen. Samuel Pratt was an early settler and landowner in Middleborough.

Philip, aka Metacom, was the son of Massasoit (real name Osamequin or Ousamequin), the Indian leader first met by the Pilgrims, and he led the Indians in the war that came to bear his name. John Eliot did lead and coordinate an effort to convert the Bible into native American languages so as to spread Christianity. John Sassamon worked with him on this project.

The Wompanoag language is a very difficult language to understand and interpret. Reliable vocabulary information is scarce. I attempted to use words that were accurate – or logically close – based upon two sources of Wompanoag vocabulary that I was able to obtain.

BIBLIOGRAPHY
(AND REFERENCES)

Books :

Kawashima, Yasuhide, **Igniting King Philip's War : The John Sassamon Murder Trial**, University Press of Kansas, Lawrence, KS, 2001.

Philbrick, Nathaniel, **Mayflower**, Penguin Books, New York, NY, 2006.

Travers, Milton A., **One of the Keys – The Wompanoag Indian Contribution**, published by the Dartmouth, Massachusetts Bicentennial Commission, Dartmouth, MA, 1975.

Weston, Thomas, **History of the Town of Middleborough, Massachusetts**, Houghton, Mifflin and Company, Boston, MA, 1906.

Websites :

O'Brien, Dr. Frank Waabu, **Bringing Back Our Lost Language**, http://www.geocities.com/bigorrin/waabu1.htm

LOUIS GARAFALO

References :

Part One

Page 1 – Waabu O'Brien website. *"Nanummattin"* = wind, north wind.

Page 3 – Waabu O'Brien website. *"Massa-ashaunt"* = "ashaunt" = lobster and "Massa" is a prefix meaning "big" or "great".

Author's note – I made this word combination up.

Page 29 – Waabu O'Brien website and also Travers. *"Wetu"* = teepee or wigwam, usually a structure that included bark siding.

Page 34 – Waabu O'Brien website. *"Wauchaunat"* = guardian(s) = wachamick = they who watch over, protect us".

Author's note – I was searching for a word that would describe an Indian who recalled the days before the English settlers arrived and chose this word as being meaningful / applicable. The logic of the connection is mine alone.

Page 35 - Waabu O'Brien website. *"Weetompain"* = a friend, kinsman, in general (singular).

Page 37 – Waabu O'Brien website. *"Mautaubon"* = day, daybreak, it is break of day

Page 65 – the legend of Mon-do-min is from Weston's **History of the Town of Middleborough, Massachusetts**,

164

Chapter 1, page 3.

Page 73 – Waabu O'Brien website. *"Taquonck"* = fall of leaf, Autumn.

Page 102 – Sassamon met with Governor Winslow in mid-January of 1675 expressing his concern about Philip's activities and about his own safety. Winslow was dismissive and, within weeks, Sassamon was murdered. Nathaniel Philbrick's version of these events is on pages 220-221 of **Mayflower**.

Part Two

Page 113 - the factual details about the trial and the hanging are taken from pages 102 – 111 of Kawashima's **Igniting King Philip's War**. The description of the scene is the author's interpretation of how it might have happened.

Unfortunately for Wampapaquan, he was executed a month later. Kawashima writes on pages 110 – 111 :

"Despite the failed execution, which usually exempted the condemned from further punishment, and a promised pardon in exchange for his confession, the Plymouth authorities were unwilling to relieve Wampapaquan. One month later, Plymouth decided to try his execution again. By then the war, which started by the skirmishes in Swansea, was already in full swing. Hanging was the only form of capital punishment sanctioned in the New England colonies, although other means of execution were employed on rare, extraordi-

nary occasions. The Plymouth authorities made sure that nothing would go wrong on the second try by shooting Wampapaquan to death."

Page 117 – after the executions Philip did convene a war council at Mount Hope and clearly had been preparing for war. The factual details come from both Philbrick's **Mayflower** and Kawashima's **Igniting King Philip's War** but the description of the scene is the author's interpretation of how it might have happened.

Page 120 – Wamsuttas' request to change their names to Alexander and Philip, plus circumstances surrounding Wamsuttas's death, are taken from Philbrick's **Mayflower**, pages 195 - 197. The scene of Philip relaying the details to Tuspaquin and Tokanauset is the author's fictional interpretation. John Sassamon <u>was</u> the interpreter referenced and was the one who initiated the legal proceedings in a Plymouth court to change their names (page 196)

Page 121 – the Metacom / Philip as "king" story is from Philbrick's **Mayflower**, page 205.

Page 122 – the story of Sassamon distorting Philip's will is from Philbrick's **Mayflower**, page 211.

Page 126 – Samuel Moseley and Cornelius Anderson were real commanders. Their description is taken from Philbrick's **Mayflower**, pages 238 – 239.

Page 134 – Amos Churchill is a fictional character.

Also By Louis Garafalo

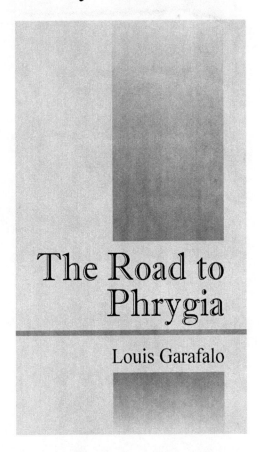

The Road to Phrygia

An exciting interpretation of the events that surrounded Jesus, Mary, Peter and the apostles during the crucifixion and resurrection of Jesus.

Learn more at: www.outskirtspress.com/Phrygia